The Case of the
Mysterious Message

The Case of the Mysterious Message

Mysteries in Odyssey

Marshal Younger

Tommy nelson™
A Division of Thomas Nelson, Inc.
www.tommynelson.com
www.ThomasNelson.com

Published in Nashville, Tennessee, by Tommy Nelson®, a division of Thomas Nelson, Inc.

This is a work of fiction, and any resemblance betweeen the characters in this book and real persons is coincidental.

Library of Congress Cataloging-in-Publication

Younger, Marshal.
    The case of the mysterious message / by Marshal Younger.
        p. cm. – (Mysteries in Odyssey ; #1)
    Summary: When Cal finds an undelivered love letter written forty years earlier, he and his friends uncover the details of a crime, a cover-up, and a romance.
    ISBN 1-56179-972-6
    [1. Letters—Fiction. 2. Love-letters—Fiction. 3. Mistaken identity—Fiction. 4. Conduct of life—Fiction. 5. Christian life—Fiction. 6. Mystery and detective stories.]
I. Title. II.
PZ7.Y8943 Cas 2002
[Fic]—dc21   2002071832

Printed in the United States of America

03 04 05 06 PHX 07 5 4 3 2

Beneath the Wreckage

hing! Ching!

"Oh no!" muttered Cal. "Not again! Not now!" Cal held his breath, topped Deadman's Hill, and headed downward fast, too fast! His bike chain dragged on the pavement beneath him. The chain had broken before—but it had never happened while flying 4,236 miles per hour down the steepest hill in Odyssey.

Sarah, who had already started down the hill ahead of him, quickly glanced back. "What's wrong?" she shouted.

"I don't have any brakes!" he yelled again. "I'm out of control!"

The bottom of the hill rushed toward him. *I've got to make the turn!* thought Cal. *I've got to make the turn!*

1

What if I don't make the turn? Big cliff! Sharp rocks! I've got to make the turn!

The handlebars shook like a jackhammer in his sweaty grip. He swallowed, and a pinecone seemed to be stuck behind his Adam's apple. A pale face zipped past on his right. It was Sarah, looking like a spectator at the Indianapolis 500.

"Cal!" she shouted, already sounding distant.

The bike's frame and gear rim banged together while the front wheel swerved back and forth. *I've got to bail out*, thought Cal. *It's my only chance to survive.*

Cal jerked his right hand back and made a quick turn. He slammed onto the curb, then bounced over it, sailing through the air for one, two, three seconds before he landed on the bike seat with a thud. "Ow!"

"Cal! Watch out!" he heard Sarah far behind him.

His bike mowed through the grassy shoulder then dropped into a wooded ravine. Trees darted past him as he tried turning right and left. "Aaaaahhhh!"

The thickening trees scraped Cal's arms and smacked his legs. *I have to roll off,* he thought. A massive tree trunk barreled toward him, bigger than a freight train. There was no way to avoid it! *Now!*

He leaped off his bike and crashed into a pile of dirt. *Wham!* The ground whacked his chest and forced out all of the air. The world spun around him and he tumbled to a stop, just as his bike slammed into the tree. Metal flew in all directions.

I would be dead meat right now if I had stayed on that

bike, he thought. He was covered in cold, grainy dirt. He spit out a clod. He wasn't quite ready to get up and determine which and how many limbs he had broken. His side ached like a bad cramp. *I'll just lie here for a couple of days,* he thought.

"Cal!" Sarah yelled in the distance. Cal watched as she stumbled down the steep ravine. "Cal Jordan, answer me!"

Cal groaned and threw up his hand. "Over here," he said, and Sarah slid to a halt beside him. Cal raised his head a half-inch and noticed Sarah's red hat. Her pale face cut through a blurry haze.

Sarah scrunched her face. "Cal! Are you hurt?"

"I don't know," he said.

Sarah brushed the leaves away from him. "Can you move?" she asked.

"I don't know."

"Have you tried?"

"I don't know."

"Well, at least move your foot," she ordered.

It took some effort, but Cal wiggled his big toe.

"Can you roll over?" Sarah asked in a motherly tone, though she was the same age as Cal.

Cal moved his arm underneath himself and, with a moan, pushed himself over. He hadn't felt this bad since Coach McGee made him run five extra laps for cutting gym class. Cal's thin body wasn't made for this kind of punishment.

He stared at the sun peeking through the branches

above him. A smile crept across his face. "That was so cool."

Sarah bopped him on the shoulder. "That was so dumb. You could've killed yourself. Can you even sit up?"

With another groan, he did. Dirt fell from his brown hair, and he spit an acorn from the corner of his mouth.

Sarah shook her head and rolled her eyes. "I told you to get that chain fixed," she said.

"I did fix it," said Cal.

"With a paper clip? That doesn't count."

Cal rolled his head around and shook his limbs. Nothing felt broken.

"You ruined your bike," said Sarah.

"It was on its way out anyway." Cal shook the cobwebs from his hair. For a moment, the world ebbed in and out of focus. Cal looked up the side of ravine.

"I've got to be the first kid ever to ride down that hill," he said. "Maybe we should leave my bike here. People can come see the wreckage. We could charge admission."

"It wasn't that impressive," said Sarah. "I could've made it down the hill better than you did."

Cal's side stung, and he lifted his shirt. He was skinned from his armpits to his waist. That seemed to be his only injury though. Part of him wished the wound was more severe—he could probably sell more tickets to the accident scene if it were.

Cal glanced down and saw something in the dirt—a flash of white metal. It was probably the thing that had skinned his side. He picked up a stick and began prodding the dirt with it.

"Hey, Sarah, look at this."

The metal was curved and disappeared into the ground. "This looks like it's been here for a while," said Cal. Sarah helped him scrape away more dirt. They saw a blue decal with the letter *U*. They kept digging and found a period, then an *S*.

Sarah found a stick and scraped away even more dirt until finally they could read the entire phrase: "U.S. Postal Service." Cal pried the metal piece from the ground, wedging his stick beneath it, and then stomping on the other half.

The metal piece was a door—a door from a mail truck, though it wasn't attached to the rest of the truck.

"There must have been an accident," said Sarah. Cal growled as he pulled on the door. It budged, and they could see an open space above the dirt.

"It must have been awful," said Sarah. "I wonder if the driver was badly hurt. I bet Mr. Whittaker might remember. He might know if . . . " Her voice trailed off.

Cal wasn't listening. His eyes fixed on something gray beneath the hood. He reached down and pulled. Like buried treasure, out came a mailbag full of letters.

Mud covered the bag, but it had been protected from most moisture by the door. Cal tugged open the drawstring and pulled out a letter. "It's a bank statement," he said. The numbers on it were quite readable.

Sarah grabbed her own handful of letters. "Look at the postmarks on these. 1962!"

"Wow!" said Cal and dug out another handful. He ripped open a hand-written letter on blue stationery. "This is so cool! It's like a time capsule!"

"Wait a minute!" said Sarah. "We shouldn't open other people's mail. It's illegal." Cal ignored her again. Sarah was being bossy, telling him what to do

"Gimme a break," said Cal, "these things are forty years old. Nobody cares about them."

"How do you know?" asked Sarah.

"Oh yeah, right. I bet there's some seventy-year-old grandmother who's been going to her mailbox every day for forty years, just hoping for this Sears catalog that never came."

"We need to take these to the post office," said Sarah. Cal ripped open a padded envelope and began reading another letter. "Stop it, Cal."

"Ooh, a love letter," he said. "Pretty romantic."

"That's enough," said Sarah. "That letter belongs to someone else. It wasn't meant for you to read." Cal knew Sarah was pretty good at judging right from wrong. But one of Cal's favorite things to do was to tempt his friends to misbehave.

"You do what you want, and I'll do what I want," he said. He read the letter to himself, but all the while he felt Sarah leaning in slowly over his shoulder. He shifted his weight so she could get a better look.

But the love letter was just the beginning.

The Other Letter

April 16, 7:12 P.M.
Whit's End, Odyssey

Cal ran into Whit's End at dusk. Whit's End was the favorite hangout for the kids of Odyssey. It had an ice cream shop, but it also had fun and educational things to do all over the place—there was a theater, a huge train set, and the Bible Room. Cal went through the front door holding the dirty, mildewed mailbag like a trophy. He figured Whit's End was the perfect place to show off his new treasure. He held the bag proudly in front of the counter.

"What's that?" Connie Kendall, a teenage employee, asked him. She had just finished scooping a triple-scoop ice cream cone and handed it to a young boy.

Cal figured Connie would react just as Sarah did, telling him to "do the right thing" and turn in the bag.

7

But he had to show someone his find, and he also knew Connie was quite the romantic too. Connie had not experienced much romance herself, but frequently lived it through others. She even had her own wedding planning service—"Dreams by Constance."

He set the mailbag on the counter in front of her.

"So, what is it?" Connie asked again.

"A link to the past," he said with a big, toothy grin.

"He thinks he's Christopher Columbus with his big discovery," said Sarah. She had slumped in behind him and now took off her cap. It left her hair matted to her scalp. Though Cal would never admit it, he thought it was pretty cool that she was a girl, and yet she wasn't obsessed with her hair.

"Well, whatever it is," Connie said, "it's getting the counter dirty. Take it off, please."

Cal pulled the bag off the counter and placed it on a chair. *She obviously doesn't know a treasure when she sees one*, thought Cal.

Sarah sat in a chair beside the mailbag. "Is Mr. Whittaker here?" she asked. Mr. Whittaker owned Whit's End. "He needs to tell Cal that he can't keep this."

"Whit's not here," said Connie. She blew her brown bangs out of her eyes and wiped a glob of ice cream off the counter.

"Where is he? Can we call him?" Sarah persisted.

"It's long distance. He's visiting his grandkids in California for the week. Why? What is it?"

Cal pulled out the padded envelope and waved it in

front of Connie's face. "It's the coolest thing you'll ever see."

"What?"

"Don't listen to him, Connie. That's how he got me to read it too," said Sarah.

"Read what?" Connie asked.

"A love letter from 1962."

"Where did you find it?"

Sarah piped in. "It was hidden under the door of a mail truck down in the ravine. There must have been an accident back then."

"And you opened up *all* of the letters?" Connie asked.

"Well, yeah," said Cal, "but most of them were boring."

Eugene Meltsner called out from the kitchen. "Opening U.S. mail that isn't addressed to you is a federal offense, punishable by a significant prison sentence." Eugene—resident genius, college student, and part-time employee at Whit's End—always had something to say.

"That's what I keep telling him," Sarah said, "but then he made me read the letter."

"How did he make you?" Connie asked.

"By holding it close to my face."

"Here, read it," Cal said and pulled the folded letter from a padded envelope that was much too large for its contents.

Eugene bolted from the kitchen like it was on fire. His glasses nearly fell off of his face when he stopped abruptly at the counter. "I must protest, Mr. Jordan. Reading that letter makes us accomplices to your federal crime. If we read it, we too will be liable to your same punishment."

"Not if I read it to you," Cal said, having no idea if it were true. He gave Eugene the same sly look he had given Sarah in the woods. "There's something else in here that looks suspicious, like the guy who wrote it was up to—" he paused dramatically, "—illegal activity. It could be an unsolved crime. We could help bring an evil criminal to justice. He's been running around loose and dangerous the last forty years!"

"Get real," said Sarah.

Eugene sighed and gave Cal a skeptical look. "You made these conclusions based on a love letter?"

"Just listen to it."

"I shan't," Eugene said, marching back to the kitchen.

Cal held the letter to eye-level, and Connie leaned forward. He was surprised she had given in so easily.

"It's addressed to someone named Rebecca Fontanero," said Cal. "And it's from Adam Barry. It was returned to Adam's address because there wasn't enough postage. Now listen." He cleared his throat.

Dear Rebecca,

I write to you with the desperate hope that you've changed your mind about me. I don't blame you if you never want to talk to me again. I know I've done terrible things. But I hope you'll find it in your heart to forgive me.

I'm leaving. For where, I'm not sure. There is nothing

for me in Odyssey now. But I will be back. Every year on the anniversary of the day we met, I'll wait at the gazebo in McAllister Park. I hope, someday, you'll meet me there.

Other than that, I won't contact you again. I promise. I don't want to pressure you into a relationship you don't want. But if you decide you want me, I'll be there, waiting for you, hoping. Hope is all I have.

The enclosed gift isn't to win you back. I only want to be able to dream of you wearing it.

I love you, and always will.

Adam

Connie shook. "I just got chills."

Sarah rolled her eyes, and Cal agreed. *That was the most disgusting letter I've ever read,* he thought.

"What gift is he talking about?" Connie asked, shaking the empty envelope.

"I don't know," said Cal. "There was nothing else in the envelope."

"This letter is so sad," Connie continued. "Adam probably went to the gazebo every year, looking for Rebecca, and she didn't even know to go there because she never got the letter." She gasped. "What if Adam *still* goes to the gazebo?"

"Unlikely," Eugene called from the kitchen. Cal smiled, triumphant that he had pulled Eugene in as well. "The man is probably in his seventies by now. I'm certain he would get the proverbial point after a decade or two. Most likely, Adam gave up on Rebecca and got married to someone else." Eugene paused and cleared his throat. "I just happened to overhear."

"But what if Adam and Rebecca were meant to be together?" Connie whined.

Eugene came out of the kitchen. "This conjecture is certainly entertaining, but I'm quite puzzled, Mr. Jordan. Why do you think that Adam Barry is a criminal?"

"I haven't gotten to the cool letter yet."

"There's another letter?"

"Yep. Right here." Cal held up a white envelope with the name "Adam Barry" typed across it. There was no return address.

"So this one was written *to* Adam Barry?" Eugene asked.

"That's right. Listen."

Adam,

Good work. I'll send you a money order for $50,000. If news of this gets out to anyone, you'll pay for it for the rest of your life . . . or perhaps with your life.

Signed,
W

Only the cursive *W* was hand-written.

"$50,000?" Connie exclaimed too loudly. She slapped her hand across her mouth when several of the patrons at Whit's End turned her way.

"The guy's a crook," said Cal.

"You don't know that," said Sarah.

"He took $50,000 to do some secret job?" said Cal. "That sounds fishy to me."

"There's no evidence that the secret job was illegal."

"Then what was it?" Cal asked.

"I don't know."

"Crook," Cal said without doubt.

"Even if it was illegal," added Connie, "maybe he knows it was wrong. He said in the letter to Rebecca that he'd made mistakes. Maybe he turned himself in."

"Oh, come on," said Cal. "Adam Barry said he was going to come back to Odyssey every year. That means he didn't plan on going to jail."

"He couldn't be a crook," Connie said. "He sounds too nice. He loved her."

"So what?" Cal asked. "Maybe he was just pretending."

"He wasn't pretending!" Connie shouted. Again, the patrons at Whit's End stared.

Eugene cleared his throat. "It makes very little difference who this Barry person was," he said, "or whether or not he was a crook or a jilted boyfriend. The fact is, all of the people involved here are at least in their sixties. They have almost certainly moved on from whatever took place in 1962, and at the very least, this is none of our business because we must immediately turn this letter in to the police and take this mailbag to the post office." Eugene took a deep breath.

"No!" Cal said. "We have to investigate this. There could be a criminal on the loose!"

"Right, Cal," said Sarah. "Like you would even be able to solve this mystery. You search your locker at school for hours for your lunch bag."

"I could solve it faster than you!" Cal said.

"Irrelevant," Eugene interrupted. "It's irrelevant. This matter should be investigated by the proper authorities, not by the four of us. Now I suggest we lay our curiosity aside."

"All right," Connie said.

Cal nodded along with her, though he didn't agree with any of it. He grabbed the two letters and slipped them back into the mailbag. *Fine. I'll just investigate this myself.*

"After I conclude my shift tonight, I will take the letter to the police station," Eugene said. "We'll leave the mailbag in Mr. Whittaker's office until tomorrow morning, as the post office is closed for the night."

"All right," said Cal, putting on his best obedient face, "I'll take it up there."

"Thank you," Eugene said, "Just put it by Mr. Whittaker's desk."

"Sure thing."

Cal pulled the heavy bag up the stairs to Mr. Whittaker's office. All the while, he glanced back to see if anyone had followed him. They hadn't.

He placed the bag inside Mr. Whittaker's door, and after one more glance behind him, he slipped the two letters out. He took them to the corner of the room and placed them on the copier. Then he pressed "Start."

At home, Cal eased into his room. He locked the door before he settled at his desk. There, he flipped on a small lamp, and in the circle of its light, he looked at a blue velvet box that snapped open at one end. Inside lay a necklace from 1962. Its round diamonds sparkled in the light, and the gold felt light and chilly as Cal picked it up.

Forty years ago, Adam Barry had placed this very necklace in an envelope for Rebecca Fontanero. Cal had found it in the ravine and stuffed it into his pocket when Sarah wasn't looking. He hadn't thought much of it until now. The gift was forty years old—who cared? Then Connie had to go and make them human—Rebecca and Adam. Two people who may actually wonder where this necklace is, may actually miss it. Cal thought, *But if I admit what I've done, they'll probably tell on me.*

Cal needed to prove that Adam Barry was a criminal. If he had stolen the necklace from a criminal, somehow his taking it didn't seem so bad. *After all,* thought Cal, *Adam probably stole the necklace himself.*

I've got to prove that Adam didn't deserve this necklace or Rebecca. At least if Cal did that, he would be able to sleep well. He didn't think he would sleep much tonight.

3
Private Investigations

April 16, 10:20 P.M.
Odyssey Police Station

he police station bustled with activity as Eugene stepped through the double doors. There were a dozen uniformed officers answering phones and filling out paperwork. Eugene was surprised by all of the activity. Odyssey was a peaceful town for the most part. Usually, the police officers in Odyssey were about as busy as the seismologists.

Eugene wrinkled his nose and held his breath a few seconds. The hallway smelled like a locker room. He was relieved to see the office of the only person on the force he knew—Captain Quinn. He wove his way through the maze of blue uniforms and knocked on the office door. Quinn was on the phone but waved Eugene in.

"Yeah, get Pinella on it," he said into the phone

16

while pacing in front of his chair. Quinn's shirttail was untucked. "I don't care if he's having a barbecue, we need him. Get him here," said Quinn. He hung up the phone. Eugene cleared his throat and stepped closer to his desk.

"What can I do for you, Eugene?" Quinn's double chin flapped slightly.

"Well, in the interest of getting right to the point, several of us at Whit's End stumbled upon a most intriguing mystery."

An officer poked her head through the doorway. "Captain," she said, "we've apprehended Rick Foster."

"Good. Is he here?"

"Right outside."

"I'll meet with him in a couple of minutes. Don't give him any coffee."

The officer nodded and left the room.

"Sorry about that, Eugene. Go on."

"Yes, um . . . We found a mailbag filled with letters from 1962." Captain Quinn raised an eyebrow. "And there were two letters in particular that caught our attention."

Suddenly, the phone rang. "Excuse me," said Captain Quinn. He picked up the receiver. Eugene stepped back and pretended to be interested in Captain Quinn's academy class pictures. He didn't want to eavesdrop on Quinn's conversation.

A few seconds later, Quinn hung up the phone and sighed. "Sorry again, Eugene," he said.

"I understand," said Eugene. "It seems quite busy here."

"Yes, it's spring break, and the Odyssey versus Connellsville baseball game is this Saturday. The kids from Connellsville always come down to shake things up. Playing pranks, you know how high school kids are."

Eugene nodded, but he actually couldn't relate. His high school experience (he graduated at age twelve) was spent in the library.

"We always have little scuffles here and there," said Captain Quinn. "Every year it's the same. So we're doubling our staff. Now what were you saying?"

"I was wondering if you could investigate this letter." Eugene handed it to the captain, who looked it over less than carefully.

"What's this about?" Quinn shook his head.

"It was sent to a man named Adam Barry, who may have been doing something illegal to earn $50,000. And there's actually another letter—"

"And you know this person?" asked Quinn.

"No, sir. I have no idea who he is."

"Adam Barry sounds familiar. Is he one of those Connellsville kids?"

"No, Captain Quinn. This letter is from 1962. Cal and Sarah found it in a mailbag in a ravine off Overlook Drive. It was presumably left there after a mail truck accident, and—" Eugene stopped. Captain Quinn wasn't looking at Eugene or the letter. He was smiling into his badge, picking lettuce from one of his teeth.

"Okay," said Quinn. "Let me get this straight. You want me to investigate a crime that may or may not have happened forty years ago?"

Eugene thought Quinn made it sound a lot sillier than was necessary. "If you deem it to be of value," said Eugene.

Quinn looked at the mess on his desk, then gave Eugene a look that said, "Can't you see I'm overworked here?"

But he didn't say that out loud. Instead, Captain Quinn said, "I'll look into it when I get the chance."

"Thank you," said Eugene. Quinn lifted the phone and punched in a number, so Eugene took this as a sign that his time with the captain was over. He backed out of the office.

"Eugene, could you shut the door for me please?" Quinn asked.

As Eugene walked past Quinn's office window, he saw the captain toss the letter onto one of the many piles of paperwork on his desk. Eugene wondered if the captain would even remember to look at it.

Eugene shook his head when he stepped outside the station. The captain's response wasn't what Eugene had hoped it would be. Eugene believed the case was worth investigating. But maybe asking the Odyssey police to make it a priority was not the way to go. *Perhaps this is something I need to do myself*, thought Eugene.

April 16, 10:40 P.M.
Whit's End

Connie had already started home for the night, but after only a few steps down the street, she found herself turning around and heading back to Whit's End. She didn't think sleep was really an option—the letters had piqued her curiosity and the possibilities were bouncing off the walls of her mind. So at 10:45 that night, she was back at the door of Whit's End.

She went straight to Whit's office and sat in his chair. There, she lifted the mailbag onto his desk. The bag held dozens of letters, bills, and advertisements. On top, Connie found the padded envelope addressed to Rebecca Fontanero. It smelled like mildew.

She opened the letter inside. Leaning back in Whit's chair, Connie read through it once more. "I'll be there waiting for you, hoping." Connie said out loud.

Every word seemed so perfect. She just knew Adam had spent hours crafting each phrase. Even his handwriting was beautiful—swirling *A's* and *T's* crossed slightly off-center.

She imagined Adam meeting Rebecca in the park, the first time in forty years. They would see each other from afar, and without a word, move closer, in their own world. And then they would embrace on the steps of the gazebo together for the rest of their lives . . .

"Miss Kendall!"

"Aahhh!" Connie jumped, banging her knees on the underside of Whit's desk. She doubled over in pain. "Owww! Eugene! Don't do that!"

"I simply said your name."

"You never say a person's name in an empty building late at night when they don't know you're there."

"Good tip," said Eugene.

"What are you doing here anyway?" asked Connie.

"A question I could very easily ask you," Eugene said. "I thought we had agreed to lay this curiosity to rest."

"I couldn't help it. What about you?"

"I . . . saw the light on. I thought there might be trouble," said Eugene.

Connie rubbed her knees. "Wait. What are you doing in this part of town? You left the shop half an hour ago."

"I was merely . . . coming back from the police station . . ."

Connie cleared her throat and smiled. "Your dorm room is in the opposite direction. You wouldn't come by here if you were going home. Just admit it. You came back to read the letter. I had no idea you were such a romantic, Eugene."

Eugene crossed his arms. "Surely you jest," he said. "I came for Adam Barry's address. I have decided to proceed with my own investigation."

"I thought we had agreed to 'lay our curiosity to rest'."

"This is not curiosity. My cause is much more important than a teenage girl's romantic notions. Besides, it appears that the Odyssey police force has more important things to do than investigate a forty-year-old crime that may or may not have taken place. So I am taking it upon myself to do so."

"Good!" said Connie. "True love between two people is so rare. And that's without mail truck accidents getting in the way."

"And just what do you intend to do about it?" asked Eugene.

"I'm going to make sure this letter gets to Rebecca. If she's still alive."

Eugene chuckled. "I admire your ambitious endeavor, Miss Kendall, but the odds of rekindling a forty-year-old romance are staggeringly slim, especially when it quite possibly involves a man who might be a fugitive criminal."

"He is not a criminal! Have you read this letter?" asked Connie.

"I am not discounting the possibility that Adam Barry is an innocent man, but justice must be served. I plan to investigate, and for lack of anywhere better to begin, I will start at the address on the envelope. May I see it?"

"372 Poplar Drive," said Connie. She didn't need to look at the envelope. "I was thinking about going there myself tomorrow."

"Perhaps you could go to Rebecca's address," Eugene suggested.

"4675 Courtland Avenue?" Connie said, again without looking. "Yeah, I think I will."

"Very well then," Eugene said. "I suppose we could conduct separate investigations."

"Sounds good to me."

"However, Miss Kendall—and I say this with all seriousness—if we are dealing with a criminal, this may be quite dangerous. Please be careful!"

Snags

April 17, 9:02 A.M.
Frampton's Pawnshop

Cal searched the phone book for "pawnshops" and found one in downtown Odyssey— Frampton's Pawnshop. It opened at 9:00, so he needed to leave his house at 8:40, since he was traveling on foot.

Cal wasn't sure exactly what he was going to do with the necklace. He felt he should at least find out what it was actually worth. The rest would depend on that.

Inside the shop, Cal stood on one side of the counter, watching a tall man study the necklace through a black eyepiece. Cal thought it looked like a magic marker cap. He waited impatiently, with his back toward the large storefront window. He feared someone he knew would pass by, and he didn't want to try to explain this.

The man's face almost touched the counter as he turned the necklace slowly beneath the eyepiece.

"I'll give you two hundred dollars," he finally said. His face popped up, and the eyepiece fell into his hand.

A lump jumped into Cal's throat. He had never seen two hundred dollars in his life. He almost screamed, "Yes! Yes! I'll take it," but he knew not to take the first offer.

"Mr. Frampton," Cal said, shaking his head. "You and I both know this necklace is worth more than that. You think you can rip me off because I'm a kid, right? Well, there's a pawnshop across town that would treat me like an adult. Now how about we get serious?"

Mr. Frampton squinted like he was studying Cal's face, trying to determine whether he really knew what he was talking about. Cal smiled with fake confidence.

Mr. Frampton threw up his hands. "Fine. Three hundred dollars."

"I'll take it!" Cal shouted, then caught himself. He cleared his throat and lowered the pitch of his voice. "I mean—that sounds reasonable to me."

Mr. Frampton stacked fifteen twenty-dollar bills in Cal's hand. *I have three hundred dollars!*

Cal left the pawnshop and screamed with delight. Thoughts of a spending spree danced in his head. But something particular stuck in his mind.

He ran down the sidewalk toward the bike shop. A red XR-3000 mountain bike shone in the store window. Cal's old bike had been destroyed in the ravine.

He needed a new bike, didn't he? *I might as well get one I like,* thought Cal. *One that goes five hundred miles an hour . . . that everyone in town will envy . . .*

April 17, 10:02 A.M.
Whit's End

Cal knew he had made it to Whit's End in record time on his new XR-3000. He wanted to ride right through the door and show it off, but he was afraid Eugene or Connie might get suspicious. He decided to wait a few weeks before showing them the bike.

Inside Whit's End, Sarah sat at the counter, and Connie and Eugene stood behind it.

Cal's heart leapt when Connie told him she and Eugene were continuing the investigation. Cal had planned to investigate things himself, but with Eugene's brain he knew they would have a much better chance of solving the mystery. "I thought you were going to drop it," Cal said.

"We reconsidered," said Eugene.

"Cool!" said Cal. "Let's get this criminal." Cal knew he couldn't ride his new bike guilt free until he proved that Adam Barry was a crook.

"He's not a criminal," said Connie. "And Sarah and I are going to prove it."

"Sarah and you?" asked Cal.

Sarah glared at him. "Yeah. You got a problem with that?"

Cal just smiled. A competition could be interesting.

"I'll take the mailbag to the post office," Connie insisted.

"Are you sure, Miss Kendall?" Eugene asked. "I fear that the temptation might be too great for you to abscond with it. You might read more federally-protected mail in the hope that you would find other letters that would allow you to play matchmaker."

Connie, arms folded, glared at Eugene. It took almost a whole minute, but Connie finally stared him down. He mumbled something about washing his hands of the whole matter, and then slunk away.

"Nice work," Sarah said, grinning at Connie as they lugged the bag to Connie's car.

At the post office, Sarah grunted as they hoisted the bag onto the counter. It landed with a loud *thunk* in front of a confused-looking clerk, a white-haired woman with glasses as thick as hamburger buns. "We found this at the bottom of a ravine on Overlook Drive."

Before the woman could open her mouth, Sarah headed off the question she figured was on her mind. "An irresponsible twelve year old opened some of the letters," she said, frowning. "You know how *boys* are."

"Oh?" the clerk said.

"They're just dense, that's all. I suppose he didn't understand he could go to jail for it."

"Well, I'll have to report this to my supervisor, but I don't imagine the irresponsible twelve year old will have to go to jail." She studied some of the addresses. "Some of these streets don't even exist anymore," she said.

"We're doing the right thing," Sarah whispered as they left the building.

"I hope so," Connie said, sighing.

April 17, 10:47 A.M.
4675 Courtland Avenue

Connie and Sarah left the post office and headed to 4675 Courtland Avenue, the address Connie had memorized. It was the address that, forty years ago, had belonged to Rebecca Fontanero.

Sarah wanted to get the jump on the investigation before the boys had a chance, and she secretly wondered if this trip to Courtland Avenue was just a waste of time. *Do people really live in the same house for forty years?* Sarah wondered. When they turned onto the street, Sarah was surprised. All the houses looked fairly new.

"It goes from 4671 to 4677," Sarah said. She squinted toward the space in between the two, as if she expected some tiny house to be hidden in the shrubs with a microscopic "4675" hand-painted on it.

Connie stopped the car, and they got out. The neighborhood was nicely wooded, with trees forming an arch over the street.

"Can I help you?" an elderly lady called from across the street. She walked toward them, wearing a heavy coat and red scarf, despite the warm spring weather.

"I wish you could," Connie said, "but it looks like the house we're looking for doesn't exist."

"Did there used to be older houses here?" Sarah asked.

"Oh, yeah, a long time ago," the lady said. "They tore 'em all down in the '80s. There was a big fire. Destroyed the whole neighborhood."

"How awful," Sarah said.

"They built these up about twelve years ago. Who are you looking for?"

"Rebecca Fontanero."

"Doesn't ring a bell. When did she live here?"

"In the '60s."

"Pretty bad odds she's still here," the lady said. "Was Fontanero a married name?"

Connie and Sarah exchanged looks. Connie said, "Probably not. We think we have a letter for her."

"Did she ever get married?"

"We don't know."

"Did she grow up in Odyssey?"

"We don't know that either," Connie said. Sarah suddenly felt her face grow red. This quest sounded sillier and sillier the longer this conversation went on.

"You're not helping me out much here," the old

woman said. "But I'll tell you what. I've got a friend who lived in Odyssey in the '60s. Knew everyone in town. Her name's Mildred, and if this Rebecca was around then, she'll know her address, phone number, birth date, and identifying birthmarks."

"That sounds great," said Sarah. "Thanks."

The elderly lady phoned Mildred and talked to her for ten minutes, like old friends getting reacquainted, before she handed the phone to Sarah. Sarah held it away from her ear so Connie could listen too.

"Hi, my name is Sarah Prachett, and we have a letter that belongs to someone named Rebecca Fontanero. We'd like to give it back to her, but we have no idea where she is. We were wondering if you might know."

The woman on the other end of the line sounded older than Moses. "Now who are you?" the woman struggled to say.

"Sarah Prachett."

"Are you Ralph's boy?"

"No."

"Whose boy are you then?" Mildred asked.

"Nobody's. I'm a girl."

"Ralph doesn't have a girl."

"I don't think you know me. I'm just trying—"

"Ralph has a boy and a cow. That's it."

Sarah pulled the phone away from her ear and looked at the woman in the red scarf. "What am I supposed to do?" she asked in frustration.

"Just ask her the question," she said to Sarah. "She's one of those that has no sense of the present, but ask her a question about the past, and she's sharp as a tack."

Sarah put the phone back to her ear. "Did you know Rebecca Fontanero?"

"Rebecca Fontanero?" She paused. "Oh, yes. Class of '55. Homecoming queen. Dated the editor of the school newspaper—Adam Barry."

Sarah smiled. "That's right! Do you know what happened to her?"

"Oh, she got married and lived in Connellsville for a while. I heard she came back, but I can't be too sure."

"Did she marry Adam Barry?"

"Oh, no. Married a man who used to sell suits. I can't recall his name now."

Sarah's heart sank for Connie, knowing her romantic notions had just taken a fatal blow. Rebecca was married—and not to Adam. But they still needed to complete this investigation. There was no time to waste. "Do you know what happened to Adam Barry?" Sarah asked.

"No. No one really talked about him. He disappeared after high school. Haven't heard a thing."

April 17, 11:10 A.M.
372 Poplar Drive

Eugene and Cal pulled up at 372 Poplar Drive. It was an interesting part of town: old Victorian houses stood tall above the trees. They were well-kept, with beautiful columns and ivy creeping up the solid brick walls. But other houses sat in the midst of them—ones that were old and run-down, some of them obviously abandoned, the weeds higher than the rotting fences around them. Though it wasn't abandoned, 372 Poplar was falling apart. The roof dipped and the paint was peeling off along the front. A rusty car was parked permanently in the gravel driveway. Eugene and Cal walked across the stones, dodging thorn bushes on each side of the car. They stepped onto the creaky porch and knocked.

A shirtless man shuffled from the back. He wore a pair of shorts, a baseball hat, and nothing else. His stomach hung below his beltline. He squinted at Eugene and Cal, looking confused. *He obviously doesn't have many visitors,* Cal thought.

"Yeah?" he said, his face coming into the light. There was a streak of mustard that ran from the corner of his mouth almost to his ear. From the looks of it, it had been a week or so since he'd shaved.

Eugene cleared his throat. "Hello, I'm Eugene

32

Meltsner, and this is Cal Jordan. I was wondering if you could help us."

"You selling something?"

"No sir, we were simply wondering if you know an Adam Barry."

The man shook his head. "I don't know who you're talking about. If this is about that convenience store hold-up, my brother had nothing to do with it. We were here that night, playing cards."

"No, this has nothing to do with that."

"Then who are you?"

Cal realized he needed to take charge. He knew how to handle the situation. Like a clever salesman, he scanned the walls of the man's house. A Chicago Cubs pennant and a team picture were tacked to a wall. "We're nobody," said Cal. "We're just a couple of *Cubs* fans, and we're looking for a guy who used to live in this house."

Eugene looked at Cal strangely.

"You guys are Cubs fans?" the man said with a gap-toothed smile. "That's great. Me too. You think they're gonna do anything next year?"

"It depends on what they do with the free agent market," Cal said with authority. "They need a lead-off hitter. But even if they get one, it's still gonna be a tough division with Houston's pitching."

Cal and the man went on for a while about the Chicago Cubs, until the man chuckled and said, "Now what were you guys looking for again?"

"A man named Adam Barry. He used to live here."

"Adam Barry. Adam Barry. That rings a bell. You know what? I got something that might help you."

The man took Cal and Eugene to his backyard down a six-inch-wide trail through the weeds. An unused lawnmower sat hidden in the tall grass as they headed toward what looked to be a cellar.

There was a metal door lying flat, an entrance into a triangular stone mound that led underground. He lifted the door with some difficulty, and then grabbed a flashlight from his garage. They headed down a steep but small stairwell.

The air was musty and smelled of mildew. The walls were covered with green growth. Canned goods lined the shelves—green beans, peas, canned meats. Cal recognized the place from a movie he saw once—it was a bomb shelter, a place for people to stay in case there was a nuclear war and they couldn't go outside.

The man shined his flashlight toward a box on the corner of one of the shelves. He pulled the box down. It was filled with newspapers.

"I thought these were kinda cool, so I kept 'em. It's fun to read through 'em sometimes."

Eugene and Cal examined the papers. They were copies of the *Odyssey Times,* dated from the early '60s.

"Is that the name you're looking for?" The man pointed to the front page, and there in the corner were the words "Adam Barry, editor-in-chief."

April 17, 12:30 P.M.
Odyssey Times *cafeteria*

The man could give Eugene and Cal no more information than that, but at least now they had something to go on. They left his house and headed straight for the *Odyssey Times*. Eugene and Cal both knew the editor there—Dale Jacobs.

"Adam Barry, yes," said Dale. Eugene and Cal were talking with him in the *Times* cafeteria. It was much like the cafeteria at Odyssey Middle School, where Cal went. The floors and walls were white and dull. The tables were attached to long benches that ran on either side of them. They were the kind that folded into the wall.

"You knew Adam?" Cal asked.

"Oh, no. He was quite a bit before my time. But his name's on a plaque outside my office. He was the editor here in the late '50s, early '60s. From what I hear, he was a pretty good one."

"Do you know why he left?" Eugene asked.

"No idea," Dale said. He took a sip of coffee, and then jabbed a noodle with his fork. "But I know who you could ask." Dale looked around the cafeteria and his eyes stopped on a man in the cafeteria line. He got up and spoke with him as he was paying for a salad.

Dale gestured toward Eugene and Cal, and the older man came over with his food.

"Cal, Eugene, I'd like you to meet Alan Tarpley. He's our news editor here. He lived in Odyssey back in the '50s and '60s. He moved away for a while, but now he's back. He might be able to answer your questions."

"Please have a seat, Mr. Tarpley," Dale said. Tarpley set his tray down across from Eugene. He was tall and lanky with a handsome white-bearded face. He looked a bit like Colonel Sanders of fried chicken fame, minus the white suit.

"I'll be happy to try and answer your questions," Tarpley said.

"Thank you, Mr. Tarpley," Eugene said. "I was wondering if you had any information on Adam Barry."

Tarpley's eyes opened wide. He looked like he had just watched Eugene bring back someone from the dead. He dropped his fork into his salad, catapulting some lettuce out of the bowl and onto Dale's lap.

"Oh . . . Sorry about that, Dale."

"That's fine. It's just lettuce."

"My . . . My arthritis has been acting up here lately. I can't seem to hold on to things anymore." Tarpley regained his composure and looked Eugene in the eyes. "Adam Barry is dead."

Something in the way Tarpley said this made Cal suspicious. *There's a story behind this that he's not telling.* Cal was happy on one point, though. *At least he won't come back for his necklace.*

36

"Oh," Eugene replied. "Do you know how he died?"

"No. I just remember reading an obituary a long time ago. Adam's been dead for many years."

Eugene said, "Well . . . we wanted to know because we found something written to him, and we were afraid he was involved in shady business dealings."

"It wouldn't surprise me if Barry was involved in something illegal. He was always known for being involved in dangerous things. In fact . . . that's probably what killed him."

5

The Note on the Door

As Eugene and Cal walked back across the *Odyssey Times* parking lot, Eugene stopped suddenly and whispered a gloomy thought.

"Alas, Mr. Jordan . . . I wonder if Adam Barry was killed," he said.

"What do you mean? By whom?"

"By Mr. 'W'."

"The guy who wrote the letter?"

"Precisely," Eugene said. "Do you remember the words he used in the letter? He said, 'If word of this gets out, you will pay for it for the rest of your life . . . and possibly *with* your life.' What if word got out?"

"Yeah," said Cal. "You may be right." He hadn't considered how serious this could get.

"I think we need to continue the investigation," Eugene said. "Even if it leads nowhere, I simply cannot allow a possible killer to go free if I can do something to bring him to justice."

Even though Adam Barry was dead, Cal agreed they should keep going. He would still feel better if he knew that Adam had been a criminal before he died. Stealing from an innocent man seemed a lot worse than stealing from a crook.

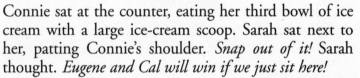

Connie sat at the counter, eating her third bowl of ice cream with a large ice-cream scoop. Sarah sat next to her, patting Connie's shoulder. *Snap out of it!* Sarah thought. *Eugene and Cal will win if we just sit here!*

"How could she marry someone else?" Connie asked. She placed her empty bowl on the counter and tossed the scoop into it. The scoop bounced out and clanged on the floor. She didn't seem to notice.

Sarah understood Connie's feelings. Connie always played matchmaker. The most tragic thing in Connie's world was two people who were "meant to be together" but couldn't work it out. Connie's parents were divorced, and "couldn't work it out," so Sarah felt sympathy for her.

"I think we should keep trying," Sarah said.

Connie didn't seem to hear her. "He was the love of her life. They were meant for each other, I know it."

The bell above the door rang, and Cal and Eugene walked in.

"We found some information on Adam Barry," Eugene said.

"I don't care," Connie said.

"He's dead," Cal blurted, stealing Eugene's thunder.

"What?" Sarah said.

"When?" Connie asked.

"A long time ago," said Cal.

"How sad," Connie said. "I've seen more romance on a box of Toaster Crunch cereal."

"However, I cannot let this case go unexplored quite yet," Eugene said.

"Why not? It's over. He's dead," Connie said.

"True . . . but there is a crime to be investigated."

"What crime?" Sarah asked.

"I believe the man who wrote the letter killed him," Eugene said dramatically.

"What?"

"'W'. Remember, he said if word of this got out, Adam would pay for it with his life."

"That's right!" said Connie.

"At any rate," said Eugene, "I feel compelled to continue our investigation. We are headed to the library."

Cal and Eugene started out, but Connie had an idea. "Hang on."

"What?"

"Wait for me," she said.

"Why?"

"I want to check on something. Let me get someone to cover for me here, and I'll be right out."

"Good idea," said Sarah, simply wanting to do something besides sit there. "Let's go check on something."

April 17, 3:43 P.M.
Campbell College Library

The Campbell College Library was an old, majestic brick building with large white columns framing the front double doors. Cal didn't like libraries much. There was always too much heavy thinking going on there.

He also didn't like the smell. The inside foyer smelled musty, of old books and magazines. The boys split off from the girls when they reached the stairs. Connie and Sarah went to the reference section on the first floor while Eugene and Cal made a beeline for the microfilm on the second. The microfilm section was a small, poorly lit room containing every copy of the *Odyssey Times* since its creation in the nineteenth century. Eugene pulled out a box labeled "Oct–Dec 1962," and they viewed it on the microfilm machine.

"What are you looking for?" Cal asked Eugene. Eugene turned a knob sticking out of the right side of the machine. Cal thought it looked like an old television set. "I'm not positive," said Eugene. "I'm hoping I'll know when I see it."

Eugene skimmed through October 1962, and the masthead on each issue read "Adam Barry, editor." Cal watched as the newspaper pages flashed by like the trees on the side of the freeway when his dad was driving fifty-five miles an hour.

Toward the middle and end of October, huge headlines read "Russians Reject Offer." Eugene said, "This was the time of the Cuban missile crisis in America."

"What was the Cuban missile crisis?" Cal asked.

"I'll explain later," said Eugene. "Right now I think we should pay attention to these headlines." The stories about the Cuban missile crisis gave way to big headlines about an election in November. An election in Odyssey and the rest of the state decided races between senators, mayors, and judges.

Nothing struck Eugene as important, so he fast-forwarded on through the rest of November. Cal waited patiently, but it felt like it did when someone else had the television remote control. Finally, Eugene stopped on April 2.

"Look at that," Eugene said.

"What?" asked Cal.

"The header." Cal looked, and on the top of the page, it read, "Merle Povich, editor."

"Adam must have quit," Cal said.

Eugene skimmed back through the issues, and finally found something striking—a smaller headline on page two—"Odyssey Times Editor Fired for Using Unreliable Source." The story talked about Adam

Barry and the end of his tenure as editor of the *Times*.

"Using an unreliable source?" Cal asked. "What does that mean?"

"Well," said Eugene. "Most likely that means Adam Barry allowed a story to be printed that turned out to be false. And whoever gave him the story turned out to be untrustworthy."

"That can get you fired?" Cal asked.

"If the right people are hurt by it," said Eugene, "I imagine it would."

Connie stood on her tiptoes and grabbed an Odyssey High School yearbook off the musty shelves. Sarah saw it was dated 1955. Connie grabbed 1954 and 1956 as well and took them to a nearby table. Sarah wondered what kinds of information Eugene had uncovered in the microfilm room. Connie blew dust off the cover and opened it.

"You're looking for Rebecca, right?" Sarah whispered.

"Yes."

"Why?"

"I just want to know what she looked like. I have a picture in my mind, and I want to see how close it really is."

Or maybe we'll recognize her, Sarah thought.

Connie flipped through the pages. They chuckled at the sight of '50s fashions and hairstyles—the boys' greased-back hair and the girls with cat-eye glasses and hair stacked to the ceiling.

Connie went to the *F*'s and landed on Rebecca Fontanero's page. "There she is." Rebecca had dark, curly hair and perfect skin. For a moment, Sarah forgot what Eugene and Cal were doing.

"She's beautiful," said Sarah.

Sarah stared at the picture for a while, like she knew Rebecca personally. Rebecca had a sincere smile, like she was naturally happy.

They found Rebecca's picture on a few more pages. Rebecca had been a cheerleader and on the student council.

Connie turned to the *B*'s and found Adam Barry. He was an average looking boy, not as handsome as many of the boys on the page around him. His smile seemed forced, almost fake. He had a rugged face and amazing eyes—light gray in the black-and-white picture. Sarah could barely take her eyes off of them. Finally, she shook off her gaze and concentrated on the opposite page.

It was a picture of Adam and Rebecca together. They were voted "Best Couple."

"Rebecca could've done better," Sarah said, losing herself in the '50s for the moment. "There are a lot more good looking guys."

"That's what makes their love real, Sarah," Connie replied. "Rebecca didn't date Adam for his looks. She was in love with him as a person."

On the page for graduating seniors, short biographies were printed for each student. Rebecca's biography briefly listed all of her school activities. There was also a personal quote: "I thank Jesus I was able to have such a great school experience and make so many good friends. I'll cherish them forever."

"Hmm," Connie said. "I guess she's a Christian."

Cal wandered over from the microfilm to see what Connie and Sarah were doing.

"What are you looking at?" he asked.

"None of your business," Sarah said, covering Rebecca's picture.

"Yearbook pictures," Connie said. "We found Rebecca. Wanna see?"

"Sure," Cal said. He shoved Sarah's hand away from the picture. When he saw the picture, his eyes grew large. He wiped them and refocused. "I can't believe it."

"What's the matter?" Sarah asked.

"This is Rebecca Fontanero?" Cal said, his eyes as wide as saucers.

"That's what it says," said Sarah.

"That's my grandmother."

"What?"

"I mean, she looks a whole lot younger here, but that's her. That's my Grandma Becky."

"You didn't know Rebecca Fontanero was your grandma?" Sarah asked.

"I didn't know that was her name before she got married. She's Rebecca Pastorini now."

"So she's still alive?" Connie asked.

"Yeah. And she lives in Odyssey."

"You're kidding!" Connie exclaimed. "Can we meet her?"

"She goes to my uncle's house in Richland on Wednesdays," said Cal. "But we can visit her tomorrow." A fresh wave of guilt overtook him. Cal thought of the XR-3000 and the new meaning it now held.

He had stolen from his grandmother.

April 17, 8:58 P.M.
Campbell College Library

Though the others had left, Eugene stayed at the library a few more hours, searching through the microfilm. After he couldn't find anything else related to the firing of Adam Barry, he finally decided to head home. His eyes were fuzzy after staring at the screen for so long.

He went to his dorm room. As he pulled out his keys to open the door, his hands and arms went limp. A note was taped to the door.

If you want to end up like Adam Barry, keep snooping around where you don't belong.

A Mysterious Death

April 18, 8:28 A.M.
Home of Rebecca Pastorini

Cal knocked on his grandmother's door, with Connie and Sarah flanking him on both sides. His grandmother was his favorite relative. All of his other relatives thought he was a troublemaker. They acted like they didn't want him around. But Grandma Becky gave him the benefit of the doubt. She always seemed glad to see him.

The door swung open and Rebecca gazed through the screen. She smiled and threw open her arms when she saw Cal. "Cal! What a wonderful surprise! I didn't know you were coming today. Oh, and you've brought some friends."

Cal introduced Connie and Sarah, and Rebecca greeted them like they were the Queens of England.

With the exception of graying hair and added wrinkles, this was obviously the same woman from the yearbook picture. The same smile that lit up that yearbook page was now, four decades later, lighting up Rebecca's neighborhood in Odyssey.

I have to tell her I took the necklace, thought Cal.

"Would you like some lemonade?" Rebecca asked. Everyone accepted, and Rebecca went into the kitchen to retrieve it. *I'll tell her after the lemonade*, Cal thought.

Rebecca's living room was decorated with old-fashioned drapes, lace cloths, and floral prints on her couch and chair. The shelves were packed with old Bibles and books on Christianity. A portrait of Jesus hung above the mantel.

Rebecca came back with three glasses of lemonade on a round tray. "So Connie, Sarah. What brings you here?"

Connie said, "We came here to see you."

"Oh, really. What for?" Rebecca said.

"We found something that's yours. And we thought you should know about it."

"What is it?"

"We don't actually have it. It's at the post office. You can probably go get it though."

"What on earth are you talking about?"

"It's a letter. From Adam Barry."

Rebecca's face went white. She wobbled on her heels and leaned on the sofa to catch her balance. She looked like she might faint.

Cal had no idea the letter would mean this much to his grandma. *Who was this guy?*

"Are you okay?" Connie asked.

"Grandma?" Cal asked.

"Yes. I'm fine. A letter from Adam Barry? Are you sure?"

"Yes. It was written in 1962."

Rebecca let out a breath. "Oh. I see. I thought you were going to say he gave it to you personally."

"Oh, no. We found the letter in an old mailbag."

"Okay. Okay." Rebecca fanned herself, regaining her composure. "Adam died in Vietnam."

"Oh," Connie whispered.

"Did you read the letter?" Rebecca asked.

Connie blushed and Sarah stared at the ground. "Well . . . yes. I'm sorry," Connie said.

"I didn't know it was your letter," Cal said, unsure if this made things any better.

"That's okay," Rebecca reassured them. "What did it say?"

"It was a love letter," Cal said.

"I see."

"Anyway," Connie said, "I thought maybe you would want to go to the post office and pick it up."

"I would. Yes. Would all of you like to come with me?"

"We'd love to," Connie said.

Cal could see it now. When his grandmother read the letter, she would ask about the "enclosed gift." *Everyone will look at me,* thought Cal. *I'll have to confess.*

April 18, 9:42 A.M.
Odyssey Post Office

Rebecca fetched the letter from the post office while Connie, Cal, and Sarah waited. She dropped the letter to her side like a lead weight, refusing to look at it. Cal grew increasingly impatient. *I just want to get this over with. I need to tell her.*

The small group walked to the park, and for the entire trip, Rebecca held the letter by her side.

Finally Cal had to ask, "Aren't you gonna read the letter?"

Rebecca breathed heavily and for the first time really studied the envelope. "Yes, I suppose I should." She sat down on a park bench with Connie and Sarah beside her. Cal sat on the grass in front of her.

"Do you mind our being here?" Sarah asked.

"No, please stay," Rebecca said. She slowly unfolded the blue stationery and read the letter. Rebecca smiled at first, then Cal noticed her eyes water and swell at the bottom lid. Cal closed his eyes tightly.

"Was there something else inside the package?" Rebecca asked.

Cal opened his mouth, but before any words came out, Connie cut in. "No. We think whatever it was may have fallen out."

And that was that. Cal didn't have to say a word. Had he been rescued? Rebecca read the letter again, and then she held it against her heart. *She's not acting like he was a criminal,* Cal thought.

"He still loved me," she said, with no emotion that Cal could recognize. "How different my life could've been if I'd gotten this letter in 1962."

"You would've gone to the gazebo?" Connie asked, her own eyes welling up.

Rebecca appeared startled, like she had forgotten Connie and Sarah were there. "Oh yes. I was in love with him."

Rebecca folded the letter back up and placed it gently into the envelope. *I can't tell her now,* Cal thought. *She's busy remembering him.*

"We were high-school sweethearts," she continued. "Best couple, according to the yearbook. We did everything together. Adam became a Christian shortly after we realized we had feelings for each other. The day he was baptized was one of the best days of my life." Rebecca smiled again.

"After graduation, we were planning to get married, but he wanted to settle into a career first. He got a job with the *Odyssey Times* right out of high school, and he climbed the ladder of success. He became the editor of the *Times* after only five years.

"We were engaged shortly after he got the job. But then . . . " Rebecca's eyes suddenly lost focus and she looked at the trees around her, "he made a mistake. He

51

used a bad source for an article. He got the story himself, didn't try hard enough to check it out more closely. The story proved to be a total lie, and Adam got fired. He was devastated. It was his dream job."

"What did he do?" Sarah asked.

"He went around the state looking for another job. But the news of what he had done made big headlines all over the place, and no one would hire him."

"What about the wedding?"

"Oh, it was almost like it was never in the plans. He changed. We broke up, and he moved away to find a job at any newspaper that hadn't gotten the press releases about his mistake. I suppose he must have written this letter after he found one."

"You still loved him," Connie said softly.

Rebecca nodded, and her cheeks reddened. "I never saw him again. He went to Vietnam in 1965. Then in '66, I got a letter from his best friend over there. He said Adam had been killed. I was devastated."

Cal didn't realize what Adam Barry had meant to his grandmother. She loved him. If she knew Adam had given her a necklace, she would treasure it forever. *But it's too late*, thought Cal. *I've sold it. Somebody else has probably bought it. Now she'll hate me. She can never find out.*

"Do you mean," Cal said, "that if you'd have gotten this letter you wouldn't have married Grandpa?"

"Oh, no. Joseph and I had a wonderful life together, Cal. I have no regrets. Your grandfather was a wonderful man, and I loved him deeply."

52

"How did Adam die in Vietnam?" Sarah asked.

"You know, I never found out. It was very strange. His best friend couldn't tell me, the Army couldn't tell me, no one had any idea what happened to him." Rebecca's mouth turned down. "Or so they said."

Sarah raised her eyebrows. "What do you mean by that?"

"By what?"

"You act like someone was hiding the truth from you. Like you don't really think he died in Vietnam."

"Oh, it may just be my imagination running away with me. But sometimes I get the feeling I didn't get the whole story about how Adam died."

"Do you think someone was trying to cover something up?" Sarah asked.

"Maybe. I don't know."

"You don't think he's still alive, do you?" Cal asked, hoping in his heart she would say no.

Rebecca remained silent and stared at her feet.

"Ms. Pastorini?" Connie whispered. "Do you believe Adam is still alive?"

Rebecca looked up. "I don't know. It just didn't add up. Too many people had different stories. "

Connie and Sarah exchanged looks. "If he was still alive, why didn't he come back for you?"

"I tried to answer that question for ten years. Then I gave up."

Connie asked, "Would you like us to try to find out for you . . . if he's still alive?"

"No!" Cal said without thinking. "I mean . . . Why would we do that, Connie?"

Connie smiled. "Because I'm a hopeless romantic. And if not for you, Ms. Pastorini, well . . . I'd like some answers myself."

Rebecca forced a chuckle. "I used to look for him in crowds." She smiled toward the sun. "I wouldn't mind your investigating. It would be nice to know for sure."

"Great," Connie said.

A horrifying thought passed through Cal's mind. *What if they actually find Adam Barry? He's gonna ask about the necklace.* All of this could come out—and his grandmother, the only person in Cal's family who trusted him—would find out he had stolen something from her. He couldn't handle that thought. No one could know about the necklace, but least of all the grandmother he loved.

"You don't want to find him, Grandma," Cal said, thinking quickly.

"Why not?"

"Because he's a criminal," Cal said with complete authority.

"Oh, Cal, get off it," Sarah said.

"He's not a criminal," Connie said.

"Why would you say that, Cal?" asked Rebecca.

"We found another letter, written *to* Adam. And it sounded like he was involved in something illegal."

"He has no proof," Sarah said. "The letter seemed pretty vague."

"Oh Cal," Rebecca said, "Adam would never have done something like that. Not when I knew him."

"You need to see the letter," Cal said.

"I can't imagine any letter convincing me that Adam was a criminal. He wouldn't hurt a flea."

"I'll prove it to you, Grandma. Eugene and I are looking into it. You don't want this guy anywhere near you."

"All right, Cal," Rebecca said. "You're very sweet. Looking out for your old Grandma."

Cal smiled. "Great. I gotta find Eugene then."

April 18, 1:00 P.M.
Eugene's dormitory room

For Cal, the trip over to Eugene's dorm room was long and slow. He had ridden his bike to his grandmother's house, but now he didn't feel like riding it anymore. He left it there and walked over.

When Cal opened the door to Eugene's small but perfectly tidy dorm room, he couldn't believe his eyes. Eugene sat in front of his computer, typing up a research paper for a class—like it was any other day!

"Aren't we going to try to find out about Adam Barry?"

Eugene acted like Adam Barry was the last thing on his mind. "I don't see a need to pursue the investigation further."

"What?" Cal asked, his arms outstretched like he was about to fly.

Eugene kept his eyes glued on the monitor. "I have a research paper to write, and I would rather not spend time on fruitless and childish detective work."

"Fruitless? This isn't fruitless. We could be on the verge of discovering something huge!"

"Doubtful."

"Listen," Cal said, putting on his best puppy-dog face. "My grandma told Connie and Sarah they could search for Adam Barry."

"Why?" Eugene asked. "He's dead."

"She doesn't think so. She thinks somebody's covering something up. But Eugene . . . what if they find him, and he's a dangerous killer?"

"I understand your concern for your grandmother, but what good will it do for us to keep investigating?"

"If I prove he was a criminal, Grandma will stop looking for him."

Eugene paused for a moment and looked back at Cal. He did a quick save of his work, then turned toward him. "There is more at stake here than you know, Cal."

Cal had no idea what this meant. *Why's today so different from yesterday?* Cal thought.

"Fine, I'll do it alone," Cal said matter-of-factly.

"You can't," Eugene said quickly, and then cleared his throat. "It wouldn't be prudent."

"What happened to you?" Cal asked. "You found something, didn't you? Something bad, and you don't want me to see it."

56

"No, nothing of the sort occurred."

"Then let me investigate myself."

"I can't let you do that."

"Why not?"

Eugene took a deep breath. "Because there may be danger involved."

"What are you talking about?" Cal asked.

Eugene wheeled his computer chair to a desk, and he picked up the piece of paper he had found on his door. Cal read it, and his mouth dropped open.

"Where did you find this?" Cal asked.

"Taped to my door. And I have concluded that we should discontinue the investigation immediately."

"But you know what this note means? It means somebody has something to hide. It means we were about to find it, and the person who wrote this knows it."

"Yes, all of those thoughts have passed through my mind since I received the note."

"We have to keep investigating," Cal said. "A crime was committed here, and if we don't keep going, somebody's gonna get away with it."

"This is not our business. We can let the police take care of it."

"You said yourself it didn't look like the police were going to do anything. And besides, the police may be in on it."

"I refuse to doubt the integrity of our police force."

Cal continued, "Who else knew we were even investigating? You told the police. We mentioned it at the newspaper. There were a couple dozen people

I told in my neighborhood, but other than that—"

"How many people did you tell?" Eugene asked.

"I don't know. Twenty maybe. They were all kids though."

"Most of whom I'm sure have parents. This note could have been written by any number of people."

"Don't you want to find out who?"

Eugene snagged the piece of paper from Cal's hands. "Yes, of course I do. But not at the expense of our safety."

Cal stopped listening in mid-sentence. "Wait a minute. What was that? Let me see the note again."

"Why?"

"I saw something when you pulled it out of my hand."

Eugene inspected it. "I don't see anything."

"Look at the back," Cal said. Eugene turned the paper over.

"I don't see anything."

"Hold it up to the light," Cal said. Eugene did.

There, cut in half, was a symbol—barely noticeable because of the faded ink. But with the light from Eugene's desk lamp behind it, it stood out as clear as day—the letter *P* with a lightning bolt running through it.

"That's half of the Electric Palace symbol," Cal said. The Electric Palace was an electronics store in Odyssey. "The *E* is missing, but that's it."

"You're right," Eugene said. "Someone wrote this note on the back of a receipt from the Electric Palace."

7 A Twist

E ugene's head swiveled back and forth. He peeked around every corner on the way to the Electric Palace. And though Cal didn't think Eugene would be of much use if someone attacked them, he was glad they were together.

At Eugene's insistence, they took back alleyways for the entire trip. In one alley, they heard something behind them. Eugene spun around in one awkward motion and assumed a karate position. "Hyah!" he yelled so loud Cal's ears rang.

"Would you cut that out?" Cal said. "There's nobody following us."

"Nevertheless, I believe taking extra caution would be to our advantage."

"Do you even know karate?"

"I have a fundamental understanding of the art, yes."

"They'd have you on the ground in five seconds."

"Hyah!" Eugene shouted again.

Cal thought it was great that Eugene was continuing with the investigation. He knew Eugene was nervous, but he also knew curiosity was a fierce beast to tame, especially when it came to Eugene. Eugene had a hard time not knowing things. To Eugene, unanswered questions were like a horrible itch.

They made it to the Electric Palace without spotting a single threatening figure. The double doors opened automatically in front of them, and they stepped inside. Ten aisles opened before them—packed with every electronic device imaginable—televisions, radios, computers, and electronic toys. Gaudy neon signs pointed out "Huge" and "Crazy" sales—most announcing 5 percent off the regular price on selected items.

The store's owner, Bart Rathbone, sat on the tile floor watching fourteen televisions in aisle five.

He jumped up when the doorbell sounded. "Welcome to the Electric Palace! Hey, did you see the specials we have on batteries here? You will not find a better price than this, I guarantee it." As he spoke, his unwashed hair bounced up and down on his head.

"I apologize, Mr. Rathbone," Eugene said, "but I'm afraid we're not here to purchase anything."

Bart threw up his arms. "Well, of course not. Why should I actually have a customer today? I mean, this is an electronics store, why would anyone need anything electronic?"

"Slow day, Mr. Rathbone?" Cal said.

"Oh no, it's been great," Bart said with sarcasm, "I had a mosquito in here only an hour ago. He didn't buy nothing either. Now why don't we cut with the chit-chat, and you can tell me what it is you want to waste my time with."

"Well," said Eugene, "we were wondering if you could assist us with a problem."

"Oh, you know, I'm real busy," Bart said.

"It will only take a second of your time."

"I got things to count, floors to sweep," Bart said, heading for the back room.

Cal knew which button to press when it came to Bart. "What if we buy some batteries?" Cal blurted.

Bart stopped dead in his tracks and turned around. "How about two packs?"

"Deal. Pay the man, Eugene."

"I currently have no use for batteries."

"I don't have any money," Cal said. "You'll use batteries."

"But I can't theorize about what size I will need in the future."

"Just pay him!"

Eugene dug into his pockets and pulled out some cash. "I suppose I might need two packs of . . . double A's, please."

Bart moved behind the register. "Now you're talkin'."

Eugene paid for the batteries, and then pulled out the receipt that had been taped to his door. "Would you happen to know who might have *misplaced* this receipt? It is dated last night, but I see no other visible information on it."

"Are you kidding me? You think after this week I actually could've *forgotten* a customer? He was the only one in here last night."

"Did you know him?"

"No."

"Did you catch his name?" Cal asked.

"Nope. But he was a tall guy, about sixty years old, but in good shape. Looked like he lifted weights. Black hair, crooked nose. Oh, and he drove a gray Cadillac. I remember that 'cause I'm gonna get a Cadillac one day myself. 'Course, I'll probably have to sell some electronics first."

"Gray Cadillac," Cal repeated.

"Oh, yeah. It was a beauty."

"Did this guy use a credit card?" Cal asked.

"Yeah."

"Do you the have the copy of the receipt where he signed his name?" Cal smiled. He knew it was wrong for Bart to show him the name on the receipt, but Bart didn't have a problem with being "wrong."

"Yeah, sure." Bart retrieved the paper. On the bottom was a perfectly signed name, reading "Milo Biltmore."

"You know him?" Bart asked.

"No," Eugene said. "Thank you, Mr. Rathbone."

Eugene searched behind trees and buildings all the way back to Whit's End.

"We have to be careful," Eugene said. "Any person could be a spy!"

"Relax, Eugene," Cal said, growing a bit irritated.

"I'm a bit concerned about the shadowy figure by the alleyway over there. It appears he has a weapon of some sort."

"Where?"

"To borrow the military description, ten o'clock."

"Eugene, that's Bernard Walton. And that's a squeegee."

Eugene squinted toward the figure. "Indeed."

Suddenly, a car came around the corner and sped toward Eugene and Cal. The tires screeched on the pavement.

"Take cover!" Eugene yelled and dove into the weeds. Cal stood on the sidewalk, frozen with both curiosity and fear. The car stopped next to him and the window opened.

"Cal Jordan?" The voice inside the car asked.

Cal approached the car with caution. He looked inside. Alan Tarpley, the *Odyssey Times* news editor, sat behind the wheel. Cal breathed a sigh of relief.

"Oh. Mr. Tarpley," Cal said.

"Is Eugene around?" asked Tarpley. Eugene peeked

out from the weeds. Seeing Mr. Tarpley, he stood up, brushed himself off, cleared his throat, and approached the car. Cal chuckled.

"You've got a clump of dirt on your glasses," Cal said.

"Ah. Thank you," Eugene said and wiped his glasses with the tail of his shirt.

"I was on my way to work," Tarpley began, "and I saw you walking. I have something for you." He leaned into the back seat and brought out a very old newspaper—a copy of the *Chicago Tribune,* dated January 14, 1966.

Tarpley leafed through the pages and found the obituary page. "Right there," he said, pointing to the first column.

It was a death notice for Adam Barry. The short article mentioned that he had been the editor of the *Odyssey Times* and said he had died in Vietnam. It didn't list any family members.

"I felt bad I couldn't help you out more at the office, so I thought I'd show you this in case you were still investigating."

"Thank you very much, Mr. Tarpley," said Eugene.

"You can go ahead and keep that paper," Tarpley said, "We've got tons of them in the basement of the *Times.* And let me know if there's anything else I can help you with," he said, closing the window.

"All right."

The car took off, leaving Cal and Eugene standing on the sidewalk.

"Well, I guess that's it then," Cal said. "He's dead."

"Yes," Eugene said. "It would appear so."

Cal recognized the look on Eugene's face—squinted eyes and tongue swirling thoughtfully around the inside of his mouth—it was the look he always had when he was thinking hard (which was pretty much all the time). "What's the matter?"

"Do you find Mr. Tarpley a bit strange?"

"Not really."

"It doesn't make sense that he would go to that trouble for us. We merely asked him a few questions. He has no obligation to us."

"Maybe he's just really nice."

"Possibly. But I can't help but wonder. I should take this newspaper to the college."

"Why?" asked Cal.

"Lab tests," said Eugene. "They can answer all kinds of questions."

April 18, 6:23 P.M.
Home of Rebecca Pastorini

In Rebecca's home office, Connie and Sarah searched every Web site they could think of. Still, they found no new trace of Adam Barry. Rebecca had watched their progress for half an hour before leaving the room. She hadn't returned.

Sarah looked up for a moment and was surprised to see that it was dark outside. She rubbed her forehead with both hands. "I don't know where else to try," she said. *If I had Eugene on my side,* thought Sarah, *I would have found something by now, and I would have beaten Cal.* But as soon as the thought flitted through her mind, she shook it off. *No, I don't need Eugene. We can solve this case by ourselves.*

The information they had found on Adam Barry was information they already had. They found a history of the *Odyssey Times,* with his name and tenure as editor. Then, Adam's name popped up again on a list of people who died in Vietnam. All of the information was dated. There was nothing beyond the '50s and '60s. Rebecca finally came back in. She had changed into a bathrobe and looked ready for bed.

"We're still looking," Connie said.

"You don't have to do that anymore, Connie," Rebecca said.

"But I'm sure we'll find something soon," Sarah said.

"Perhaps you will. But stop anyway. I've made a decision."

"What?"

"My life was going on very well without Adam Barry, but now you've made me so curious, I have to know. I have so many questions. So I'm going to give it one try and only one try."

"How?"

"I've written a letter to send to *America Today.*"

America Today was a national newspaper. Rebecca placed a piece of peach-colored stationery on the desk in front of them. She had written it in fancy cursive.

My name is Rebecca Fontanero Pastorini, and I am searching for a man named Adam Barry. I was told he died in Vietnam almost forty years ago, but I now have reason to believe that he is still alive. Mr. Barry was the editor of the Odyssey Times *in the 1960s.*

If you know where he is, please give him this message: I will be at our "special place" on Saturday, April 20, at 9:00 in the morning. Adam, please meet me there. If anyone knows anything, my e-mail address is FONTANEROS@GOL.com. Thank you.

Rebecca Fontanero Pastorini

Connie looked up from the page, her mouth wide open.

"I'm going to run this as a half-page ad in tomorrow's paper," said Rebecca.

Sarah loved the idea. *Why jump through all these hoops to find Adam Barry when we can just go to Adam Barry himself! Brilliant!*

Rebecca continued. "If I get a response, great. I'll be very happy to see Adam again. If I get no response, that's fine too. I'll live my life with unanswered questions. I'd already resigned myself to that anyway." Sarah didn't care for Rebecca's casual attitude. This might very well work, but if it didn't, the search had to continue.

Rebecca picked up the paper. "I'll call the newspaper now. Is there anything I should change?"

Connie and Sarah smiled at her. "I think it's perfect," Connie said.

"So do I," Sarah repeated.

April 18, 10:23 P.M.
Home of Cal Jordan

For the third night in a row, Cal couldn't sleep. *What if my grandmother actually found Adam? What if they decided to meet?* He pictured the scene over and over in his head. After an opening embrace and some small talk, Adam would say, "I was hoping you'd wear your necklace."

Grandma would say, "What necklace?"

Then it will all come out, Cal thought. *Adam tells her about the necklace, then Sarah, standing nearby, puts two and two together and asks me if I saw a necklace in the package. I'll lie, but Eugene or somebody will pry some more. Adam, confused, will get the padded envelope from the police station, and there is no evidence of any holes where the necklace could've fallen out. The impression of a velvet box is still in the inside of the package. Then they will all look at me . . . and know.*

The Gray Cadillac

8

Home of Cal Jordan
April 19, 10:37 A.M.

The next morning, the phone ringing awakened Cal. In a sleepy stupor, he lifted the receiver. "Hello?"

"Cal, this is Grandma Becky. Did I wake you?"

"Yes."

"Well, Cal, it's 10:30 already."

"I didn't get much sleep last night," Cal said, still not quite sure whom he was talking to.

"I see. Well, I wanted to tell you that you left your bike over here yesterday."

Mention of the bike startled Cal. He sat up straight in bed. Before he could say anything, his grandmother cut him off. "It's a nice bike. Looks new. Did your dad get it for you?"

"Um . . . " Cal usually had no trouble lying, but this was his grandma. Cal hesitated, trying to figure out what to say.

He didn't have to answer. "I can tell you're not awake yet," Grandma said. "I'll let you go."

"All right. Bye, Grandma."

She hung up. *That's it,* Cal thought. *I can't take this anymore. I'm going to get the necklace back. I'll take it to her and tell her it fell out in the mailbag. She won't question me. She trusts me.*

Cal jumped out of bed and threw on the first clothes he spotted.

Cal got the bike from his grandma's house and rode it as fast as he could to the bike shop where they graciously gave him his money back. After all, Cal had barely ridden the bike. It still looked very new. Next, he ran as fast as he could to the Frampton's Pawnshop. *Please,* he thought. *Oh please, let the necklace still be there.*

Inside the pawnshop, Cal scanned the full jewelry case. He looked for the round diamonds. And there they were. Cal's heart leapt. He took out the money from the bike and headed for Mr. Frampton.

"I want to buy that necklace back," he said.

"Couldn't bear to part with it, huh?" Mr. Frampton fiddled with a key ring packed with dozens of keys. He found the right one and opened the case. "Do you have $500?" he asked.

"What?" Cal said. "But you only paid me $300 for it!"

"It's worth $500 now."

"It went up 200 bucks in two days?"

"That's right."

Cal thought he had gotten a good deal. But now he realized Mr. Frampton had gotten the better end of the deal. Cal stiffened his upper lip. "I'll give you 350." *Of course, I have no idea where I'll get the extra fifty dollars.*

"No deal. Five hundred firm."

"You can't do this!"

"You see that sign out there?" Mr. Frampton asked. He pointed to the sign out front that read "Frampton's Pawnshop." "Well I'm Frampton. And that sign means I can do pretty much whatever I want."

Cal left the pawnshop with his head down. Every step he took he kicked the sidewalk with his toe. *What am I gonna do now?*

He glanced into jewelry stores on the way through town, but everything that looked remotely like his grandmother's necklace was way too expensive for him. And he knew if he bought a cheap one, that both his grandma and Adam would know the difference. Cal spent the rest of the morning and part of the afternoon looking at jewelry he couldn't afford.

April 19, 4:00 P.M.
McAllister Park

Cal's only hope was to do everything he could to keep his grandma from meeting with Adam. As he walked through McAllister Park toward Whit's End, Cal spotted Eugene.

"Your grandmother is running a half-page ad in *America Today*," said Eugene. "She's trying to find Adam Barry."

"An ad in a national paper? Isn't that a little crazy?"

"Personally, I agree with you," said Eugene. "Considering the threat I received, we could be dealing with a very shady sort. I think we should do everything we can to stop this meeting."

"Right. So where are you going?"

"Whit's End."

Suddenly, from around a far corner, Cal spotted it. A gray Cadillac. *Was it the guy Bart Rathbone had talked about?* It circled the park. Then about two hundred yards away, it stopped and swerved awkwardly to park on the side of the street.

"He saw us," Cal said. The driver's side door opened.

"Run!" Eugene shouted.

They took off through the park, toward the woods behind Whit's End.

Cal raced ahead of the awkward Eugene. He glanced back for a moment, and his worst fear was realized. A man in a blue windbreaker was chasing them!

Cal dodged around rocks. *I'm running for my life,* he thought. Eugene, out of wind after thirty feet, huffed and puffed behind him.

"Where are we going?" Cal shouted.

"This way!" Eugene said and shot out in front of Cal. Cal felt a sharp pain in his side—the injury from his bike wreck.

He dropped behind Eugene, looking back to see the man breaking into a full sprint. "He's coming!"

Eugene turned a corner around a thick veil of brush. "Can you still see him?"

"No!"

Cal saw that Eugene had a plan, but he couldn't imagine what it was. The man was gaining on them, and Eugene was heading toward the park on the other side of Whit's End—where there was no place to hide!

Suddenly, Eugene dove to the ground next to a square piece of wood imbedded in the ground. "In here!" he shouted and lifted it up.

Cal was amazed—it was a tunnel! He took a quick look to see if the man was watching. He wasn't in sight. Cal dropped into the tunnel, scraping himself on the side of the metal wall.

Eugene threw himself down the shaft and quickly pulled the door down above him.

A moment of eerie silence enveloped the room as they listened outside. The tunnel was pitch black except for a thin line of light around the door. Cal pasted his hand to his mouth, trying to hold back his breath as much as he could.

Quick footsteps approached from outside. They were coming closer. The feet shuffled leaves around, then slowed down and stopped. Cal pictured the man rotating in place, searching in all directions. The footsteps started again, breaking into a jog, and then a run . . . farther and farther away . . . .

They were safe.

Cal breathed for the first time in minutes. Eugene wiped sweat from his forehead and reached toward the wall and flipped a light switch. Red lights illuminated a hallway that disappeared around a turn.

"What is this?" Cal said, fascinated.

Eugene caught his breath long enough to explain. "It's a tunnel that leads to the basement of Whit's End."

"Cool! I didn't know this existed!"

"It was used by runaway slaves as part of the Underground Railroad during and prior to the Civil War."

"You gotta be kidding me."

"Come on."

They made their way through the tunnel to another door. Eugene pushed it open, and they found themselves in the basement of Whit's End. It was a large, dark, dusty room with old relics lining the walls and shelves. Hundreds of books, an old typewriter, and a hand-drawn map of Odyssey filled the room. There were drawings on the wall, along with blueprints of new inventions. On the desk lay half-finished contraptions.

"This is so cool! I've never been down here!"

"I'll call the police," Eugene said, moving toward a phone on the wall. "I think it would be wise of us to stay down here until they come. Will you go lock the basement door there?"

Cal obeyed.

"To borrow the colloquialism," Eugene said, "it's time to dig in."

Crisis in 1962

April 19, 4:10 P.M.
Home of Rebecca Pastorini

B y mid-afternoon, Rebecca had sixty-three new
e-mail messages, and Sarah was thoroughly
amazed. One by one, Rebecca, Connie, and Sarah
read each message. Most of the messages were pranks. A
couple of people knew an Adam Barry, but it was not the
Adam Barry they were looking for. The Adam Barry
mentioned in several e-mails was much too young, even
to have fought in the Vietnam War.

A couple of people knew Adam Barry when he was
the editor of the *Odyssey Times,* but they didn't have
new information about him.

Connie sighed. "I'm getting the feeling we weren't
meant to find him."

"We'll find him," Sarah said.

April 19, 4:15 P.M.
Basement of Whit's End

A knock on the basement door startled Cal. He looked up the stairs and a voice penetrated the door. "Eugene? Are you down there?" It was Captain Quinn. Eugene had called the police to tell them about the man who had chased him and Cal.

Eugene scrambled up the stairs to open the door. "Officer Quinn. I'm glad to see you."

Quinn shook his head. "We didn't find anyone around here, Eugene. We searched the whole area."

"Is it safe to come out?" Cal asked.

"I don't see why not. We'll keep patrolling the area. I'll send a car around every so often."

Quinn left after searching every floor of Whit's End.

Eugene walked up the stairs to Mr. Whittaker's office. Cal followed. "Are you staying here?" Cal asked.

"There are a few things I'd like to do before I go," Eugene said. He sat down at Mr. Whittaker's desk, grabbed a pen, and wrote something down on a yellow legal pad.

"What are you writing?"

"Nothing of any consequence. I'm attempting to make sense of all of this, but none of my theories are connecting." Eugene looked at Cal seriously. "We have to find out with whom we are dealing. We have breached some kind of security in their eyes, and I'm afraid they are not going to stop looking until they find us. I feel I must go on the offensive and find out as much as I can."

Cal nodded. "We need to find out about the owner of that Cadillac."

"Yes. Milo Biltmore. I'll check the Internet." Eugene turned on the computer in front of him.

He found a search engine and typed in "Milo Biltmore." Seventeen items popped up.

"That one," Cal said, pointing to one that read "Chicago Tribune." Eugene clicked on it.

The newspaper article was dated September 14, 1962, and dealt with an upcoming election being held at that time. The *Chicago Tribune* endorsed a candidate named Bill Perriman, up for election as a state senator. "I know who Bill Perriman is," Eugene said.

"Who?"

"He's a U.S. senator. And he may be the next vice-president of the United States."

Eugene scanned the page and found Milo Biltmore's name.

"The emphasis of our campaign is building up the military. We believe in protecting our people, and I don't think our current military service can do that in these uncertain times," says Perriman's campaign manager, Milo Biltmore.

"So Milo was a campaign manager," Cal said.

"Let's go to the others," Eugene said. One article listed Biltmore as Perriman's campaign manager years later, when Perriman ran for U.S. senator and won.

"So you think this senator guy has something to do with this mess?"

"I don't know," said Eugene. "But I get the distinct feeling this is getting more and more serious, Mr. Jordan."

April 19, 5:02 P.M.
Home of Rebecca Pastorini

More e-mails came in, with twelve popping up in an hour. Again, most of them were pranks, and a few of them contained information they couldn't use. Sarah rested her head in her hands, hours of frustration behind her and probably many more to come. She desperately wanted to quit but knew that Cal was still hard at work on his end. *He can't beat me,* she thought.

But then, they read one that was different. Sarah's interest was piqued for the first time in hours. The subject line read "Odyssey Times, October 28, 1962." Connie opened the e-mail. It was a transcript of a newspaper article.

"Kruschev agrees to truce, but Russian soldiers do not," Connie said, reading the bold headline out loud. "What is this about?"

"Oh, what a terrible time that was," Rebecca began. "It was the Cuban missile crisis."

"I've heard of it," said Sarah. "What happened?"

"In October of 1962, the United States discovered that Russia was placing nuclear missiles in Cuba, which is, of course, very close to our border. They were aimed directly at us. If they launched any of these missiles, they could've easily wiped out entire cities in the United States."

"Wow," Sarah said under her breath.

Rebecca went on. "So obviously, President Kennedy wanted to get rid of them. He asked Russia to move the missiles, but they refused. Then Kennedy did something so risky that it put the entire country in danger. He set up a blockade of ships to surround Cuba so that no more Russian missiles could get through. This, of course, made both Cuba and Russia very angry.

"For two weeks, America was on the brink of war, until Kruschev, the Russian leader, finally agreed to remove the missiles."

"But this article says that even though Kruschev agreed, the soldiers didn't," Connie said.

"Yes," Rebecca said. "According to this, the Russian army decided to ignore Kruschev's orders. They refused to give up the missiles. This article made us all think that America could still be close to a major war."

Sarah listened intently. History usually bored her but hearing it from someone who had actually lived through it was different.

"That was a horrible two weeks," Rebecca explained. "Everyone thought it was going to be the beginning of World War III. There was a bomb shelter in our neighbor's backyard, and I remember sitting in there for hours, listening to the radio until the batteries ran out, praying to God to protect us but expecting at any moment to be attacked."

"But," Connie said, "what does this article have to do with Adam?"

"No one knew where it came from, because no other newspaper or news station had the story—and Adam never told anyone where he got it. This is the article that got him fired."

Connie called Eugene at Whit's End and read the article to him over the phone.

"That's very strange," said Eugene.

"Why?" Connie asked.

"I don't remember anything about Russian soldiers' disobeying Kruschev."

"That's the thing," Connie said. "Rebecca said this is the article that got Adam fired. So maybe he got his facts wrong."

"But the article *I* read said Adam had used an unreliable source," Eugene said. "What is the name on the byline?"

"The byline?"

81

"Who wrote the article?"

"Oh. Yeah. Um . . . Martin Jasper."

"Okay. I'll research that name and see if I can come up with anything."

Connie and Sarah were taking a lemonade break in the kitchen when Rebecca, frantic, called out from the office. "Come here! Quick!"

They ran in. "What is it?"

Rebecca was staring at the computer. Her face was pale when she turned toward them. "Look at this one."

Connie and Sarah studied the screen and saw a new e-mail from "ADB1937@GOL.COM." It read:

Dear Rebecca,

I'll be at the gazebo, tomorrow at 9:00.

Love,
Adam

10 The Connection

"It could be a joke," Rebecca insisted. She stood up from the chair and turned away from the message on the screen.

"How could it be a joke, Rebecca?" Connie said. "He knows where your secret place is—the gazebo!"

"Plenty of people from high school knew about our special place. It could just be a terrible joke."

"Does his e-mail address mean anything to you? ADB1937?"

"Yes. Those are Adam's initials and the year he was born."

Connie smiled at Rebecca, watching her pace around the room in circles. Sarah sat at the computer investigating the note once again.

"Are you going to the gazebo?" Sarah asked.

"Of course I am."

"Then you'll find out for sure tomorrow."

"I suppose I will." Rebecca looked into Sarah's eyes. "Good heavens, what if it really is Adam? What will I say to him?"

April 19, 7:32 P.M.
Basement of Whit's End

Eugene typed "Martin Jasper" into the Associated Press search engine.

"Tell me again why we're searching this site?" asked Cal.

Eugene drummed his fingers on the desk while the computer searched the site. "Jasper wrote the article that got Adam fired," he said, "and that article listed Jasper as a reporter for the Associated Press. It's a service used by newspapers across the nation. Even the *Odyssey Times*."

"Okay," said Cal. "I think I get it now."

"Good," said Eugene. "But these results are problematic." He stared at the computer's screen. "It appears that there is no such person. Jasper isn't listed here at all."

Cal leaned back in his chair. "Maybe Adam invented the guy completely," he said.

"That doesn't make any sense," Eugene took off his glasses and rubbed his eyes. "I'm sure Martin Jasper was a fraudulent writer. He made an unfortunate joke, and Adam fell for it."

"Why would Adam accept a news story from some-body who he didn't even know?"

"That I cannot answer. But it simply makes more sense than the alternative."

"Which is?"

"That Adam simply manufactured the story himself."

"But why would he make up a story about Russian soldiers refusing to take orders?"

"I don't know."

"Maybe he was just crazy."

"Maybe this entire case is."

Sarah felt like she should rescue Rebecca from Connie. Rebecca was changing into the fifth outfit Connie had helped pick out. She emerged from the closet in a pale green dress trimmed in gold. Connie tapped her lips with her index finger. "It's not quite right," she said, shaking her head slowly. "Let's try a different color."

Connie walked into the large closet and pawed through the remaining dresses. Rebecca shrugged, and Sarah rolled her eyes. Sarah sat on the corner of the queen-size bed. The lights were as bright as they could be—part of Connie's orders.

Sarah watched as Rebecca turned in front of the mirror. She looked happy. Suddenly, it didn't matter to

Sarah if she solved the case before Cal. Besides, Rebecca was his grandmother.

"What do you want to communicate with this meeting?" Connie asked from the closet. "Because your dress selection will communicate it better than words."

"I'm not trying to communicate anything," Rebecca answered.

"Of course you are," said Connie. "What mood do you want to express?" She came out of the closet with her arms full of clothes. "See," she said and held out a red skirt. "This says, 'I'm daring. I'm bold.' But this—" Connie held out another skirt—a pink one this time. "This says, 'I'm coy yet sensitive.'"

"Connie," Sarah interrupted. "Let her wear what she wants."

"Yes, please," Rebecca agreed. "I'm not in high school. Sixty-five year olds don't play games. They wear clothes because they're comfortable."

"How about the blue one?"

"That's my daughter's dress that she left here. I couldn't fit in it if you stitched two of them together. I'm wearing this green one."

"Oh, Rebecca, no offense, but don't you think the green one is a little old-fashioned?"

"So am I. I appreciate your trying to make this into a special moment, Connie, but I think it's best if I just relax and be myself."

"Yeah, I know," Connie admitted. "But I want this to go perfectly."

"So do I," Rebecca said.

Connie stopped looking at the dress and instead looked at Rebecca, who was moving her hands nervously across her dress. Her expression was tense. "Are you okay?"

"I'm fine," Rebecca said.

"This is really hard for you. I mean, I've been so caught up in the romance of this, but this is really big for you, isn't it?"

"Yes, it is." Rebecca looked at the mirror, fiddling with the sleeves of her dress, and Connie stopped her, gently holding her hand.

"Rebecca . . . would you like to pray?"

Rebecca took a deep breath and smiled sheepishly, as if she was embarrassed that the thought hadn't occurred to her until now. "Yes, Connie. I would."

April 19, 8:15 P.M.
Basement of Whit's End

Cal watched as Eugene checked other search engines, still looking for a Martin Jasper.

"I'll walk you home in a few minutes, but I'd like to investigate one more thing," Eugene said.

"What?"

"Senator Bill Perriman."

"You mean the guy Milo Biltmore worked for?"

"Precisely. I have a feeling there is a connection between Senator Perriman and this case."

Eugene did another search, this time for Senator Bill Perriman. Thousands of references popped up.

"You don't plan on looking through all of those, do you?" Cal asked.

"No. I simply want to see if this leads anywhere."

Eugene clicked on a link, and it displayed a recent newspaper article titled "Vice-Presidential Nomination Still up for Grabs." Bill Perriman was listed as one of the people being considered for vice-president. There was a small black-and-white photo of him, a gray-haired man with a square jaw and glasses.

"Perriman could be our next vice-president."

Cal wasn't following. "Okay, fine. But what does that have to do with this case?"

"I'm still trying to figure that out."

April 19, 9:09 P.M.
Behind Whit's End

As Cal and Eugene left Whit's End, Cal remembered what Captain Quinn had told them—a police car would patrol the area to make sure everything was okay. Cal didn't see a car though, just the empty street. The wind howled around them.

"What's wrong, Cal?" asked Eugene.

Cal glanced behind him. "Maybe we should go back through the tunnel."

The tunnel door creaked as Cal closed it. Darkness hung over the woods like a black veil. Cal didn't like the dark, but the streetlights in front of Whit's End made him feel too exposed. At least they could hide in the darkness. *Biltmore will be on the street, in his car. We have to go out the back, take the long way home.*

They walked on through the woods. Cal hoped Milo wasn't hiding behind a tree. He followed closely behind Eugene, and they felt their way around trees and low-hanging branches.

Cal heard a crinkling noise from behind a bush in front of him. They both stood silent for a moment, listening intently. The wind howled through the tops of the trees, and an owl hooted a low chorus of notes. Cal moved on.

They finally emerged from the woods onto a residential street. "Where are we?" asked Cal. Eugene shrugged his shoulders. They made their way along the road until they saw a street lamp. It shone at the intersection of two streets. Cal recognized the street names—they were only a few blocks away from his house. Cal felt comfortable crossing the street and heading into a residential neighborhood.

Eugene walked Cal to the front door of his house. Cal

turned to Eugene before he went in the front door. "So I'll see you in the morning then?"

Eugene sighed. "Yes."

"Do you think my grandma's gonna be okay?"

"I certainly hope so. But I cannot begin to predict what will happen if Adam comes to the gazebo tomorrow."

Cal didn't think he would sleep tonight either.

The Missing Piece

April 20, 7:04 A.M.
Eugene's dorm room

A phone call awakened Eugene the next morning.
"Eugene, this is Jeannie down at the lab."

"Oh, hello, Jeannie. Thank you for calling. Were you able to do the lab work on the newspaper I gave to you?"

"Yeah. Where did you get this?"

"Alan Tarpley from the *Odyssey Times* gave it to me."

"It's totally fake."

"What do you mean?"

"I mean the paper itself is old, probably forty years old, but the ink is brand new, like it was printed yesterday."

"Hmm," Eugene said, scratching his head, "Thank you, Jeannie. I'll speak with you later."

Eugene hung up the phone, then dialed another number. "Cal?"

"Yeah?" Cal said groggily, obviously just waking up.

"I apologize for the inconvenient earliness of this call, but I thought I would tell you where we're starting today."

"Cool. Where?"

"The *Odyssey Times*. Alan Tarpley knows something, and I'm going to find out what it is."

He only had two hours to figure it out.

Sarah went to Rebecca's house at 7:30 that morning. She worried that she'd wake Rebecca up when she knocked on the door, but Connie had already been there for half an hour.

Connie was busily choreographing the meeting. "Which shade of lipstick are you wearing? What will be your first words? Will you hug him? How are you going to stand?"

Rebecca excused herself to go to the bathroom.

"Are you sure you're not making her more nervous?" Sarah asked Connie.

"It'll make her feel much better if this whole meeting was scripted," Connie assured her.

"Can you maybe just let me wing this?" Rebecca called from the bathroom.

"Wing it?" Connie asked with utter shock.

"Yes. I'd rather just let whatever is going to happen, happen."

April 20, 8:22 A.M.
Odyssey Times *building*

Cal and Eugene walked into the *Odyssey Times* lobby. They scanned the directory and found Alan Tarpley's office on the fourth floor.

Cal's brain had fallen two or three steps behind Eugene's as far as figuring out this case. When they got into the elevator alone, he began to ask questions.

"What do you think Tarpley knows?" Cal asked.

"I don't know," Eugene said, "but Tarpley does not want us investigating this case."

"Do you think he's the one who told Milo Biltmore to follow us?"

"It's possible."

"What do you think he'll to do to us when he finds out we're still looking for answers?"

Eugene glared at him, but he didn't have to answer. The elevator doors slid open.

The two meandered through a maze of empty cubicles toward the offices along the far wall. Eugene said, "I would assume that the news editor would have an office with walls, as opposed to a cubicle."

He was right. The corner office had a nameplate on the door reading "Alan Tarpley, News Editor." The office was empty.

"He's not here," Eugene said.

"The door's open. Let's check out his office," Cal said and moved toward the crack in the door.

"You jest," Eugene said. "We can't simply break into an office."

"Why not? The door's open."

"No. I refuse to . . ." His voice trailed off when Cal barged into the office. "Mr. Jordan, you cannot be in here."

Cal, without even looking around to see if anyone was watching him, rifled through papers on Tarpley's desk.

"We could face a jail sentence for this," Eugene pleaded.

Stapled groups of papers, magazines, newspapers, and memos with the header "Odyssey Times" on them covered the desk. Just then, Cal saw it. In the corner of the room was the fax machine and a curled up letter in the box underneath it. Somehow, before he even read it he knew the importance of it.

He stumbled around the desk and grabbed the letter from the box.

"Mr. Jordan, I cannot allow you to read other people's personal—"

"Shh!" Cal said. "Listen to this."

Alan,
Milo has failed. I am coming to Odyssey myself. I land at 8:37 A.M. this morning. If I'm not in town by 9:00, stall them.
Signed,
W. P.

"W.P." Cal said.

"Look at the *W,* Cal. It's in the same handwriting as the one in Adam's letter."

"But who is it?"

Eugene squinted. "W. P. . . ." His eyes widened. "William Perriman!"

"Bill Perriman? The senator?"

"Possibly our next vice-president."

"And he's coming here," Cal said. "We gotta tell my grandma."

"Let's go."

They stumbled over each other to get out of the office. Employees filed in. Eugene and Cal came to an abrupt halt and began to walk casually. They received some stares but made it to the elevators without being questioned.

As they waited for the elevator, Cal's brain tried to process more information than it could contain. "Okay, I'm not sure I get this," Cal said. "If Perriman was the one who sent Adam that letter, why did he pay Adam fifty thousand dollars?"

"Well, this is all speculation, but I believe this fax confirms what I suspected. William Perriman was running for State Senate in 1962. He ran on a campaign promoting a strengthened military, and when the Cuban missile crisis hit the United States, I'm certain his popularity rose."

"Why?" Cal asked, trying to follow.

"Because everyone wanted a big military to protect them because they were afraid of war."

Cal nodded.

Eugene went on. "The United States set up their blockade of Cuba in 1962. Americans lived in fear every day. Families hid out in bomb shelters across the nation. But then, in late October, just weeks before the election, Kruschev of Russia agreed to take away the missiles, and it looked like the conflict was ending."

Eugene took a breath, then continued. "Perriman panicked, because he thought that if everyone felt at peace about the conflict his popularity would suffer."

"Because he was so big on having a strong military," Cal said.

"Correct."

"And if people weren't scared anymore, they wouldn't care about a strong military."

The elevator doors opened, and they stepped into the empty elevator. "Exactly. So Senator Perriman paid Adam Barry to write a false story saying the Russian military had refused to hand over the missiles. He hoped people would think the crisis hadn't ended. Adam printed the story, got paid, the people believed they were still in danger, and Perriman was elected two weeks later. The *Times* fired Adam for the false story. Then he disappeared, fought in Vietnam, and now he is back, living in the United States again."

Cal said, "So if the real Adam Barry is coming to the gazebo, and William Perriman is too . . ."

"Perriman would do anything to prevent this story from becoming public after all these years.

He's campaigning to become our new vice-president! If this news got out, no one would vote for him!"

"But what about Alan Tarpley?"

"For some reason, I'm convinced that Perriman is paying him to keep us quiet. And he'll do anything to keep it quiet as well."

"So maybe Alan Tarpley is going to be at the gazebo too?"

"Precisely."

Cal felt a lump in his throat. His grandma was in very real danger.

They had pressed the button to go to the lobby, but on the second floor, the elevator stopped. The doors slid open, and a figure blotted out their view of the hallway. Cal stopped breathing.

It was Milo Biltmore.

The Meeting

April 20, 8:46 A.M.
McAllister Park

Sarah looked at her watch. She, Rebecca, and Connie stood on the mounted cement octagonal floor of the gazebo, in the middle of McAllister Park. White trellises outlined each side, with green ivy climbing up wood. It was the perfect setting. Rebecca looked beautiful. Sarah glanced around, waiting for someone to drive up, or walk up, or ride up on a white horse and carry Rebecca away. She shook herself out of it. *Mushy stuff. I'm starting to sound like Connie.*

Rebecca sat on the bottom step of the gazebo and tapped her heel on the ground.

Connie paced back and forth.

It was almost time.

Milo Biltmore stood in the hallway outside the elevator. He wore the same windbreaker as when he had chased Cal and Eugene into the woods. He looked to be in his sixties but stood as tall and menacing as a sixty year old could possibly stand. His jet black hair had absolutely no gray; his muscles were obviously used with regularity. He had a scar above his right eye. *He looks more like a bodyguard than a campaign manager*, Cal thought.

Cal tried to see into the hallway beyond where Milo stood, but there didn't seem to be anyone around to hear him scream.

"You two act like you're in a hurry," Milo said.

"We are," Cal said. "We're trying to get to the baseball game."

"Oh, really. I'm going right by there. Maybe I can give you a ride."

Milo stepped forward and reached out his hands to grab them. In a split-second, Cal and Eugene made eye contact.

"Run!"

Cal and Eugene ran to either side of him. Milo tried to grab them, but was too slow. They cleared Milo's range and dashed toward nothing in particular.

They were on the production floor, with huge, noisy machines churning out newspapers at a mind-boggling pace. Cal led the way and ducked behind one, then hopped over electrical cords and squirmed under conveyor belts. Somehow, Eugene made it through himself. Cal spotted a door labeled "Archives." He sprinted for it. Eugene was still behind him.

Thankfully, the door was not locked. They rushed in. It was a mammoth room, with aisles as far as the eye could see and an infinite number of shelves stacked high to the ceiling.

Off they sped, down the aisle and into the boxes. Cal heard quick footsteps behind them, but he didn't look back.

He made a sharp turn around the end of the shelves, his shoes sliding on the ground like roller skates.

They searched for another way out. Cal's eyes scanned the walls down every aisle as they whizzed past them, but found no door. He picked an aisle and took it. He looked back, and saw Eugene's terrified face, his hair flopping down into his eyes. Cal ran hunched over to look between the boxes at the next aisle. There was no one there.

He saw a door. "There!"

They sprinted for a fire door with a red arm on it that read "Alarm will sound." *Perfect*, Cal thought. *The police will arrive and save us.*

Cal moved faster than he had ever moved in his life. He held up his arm to burst through the door.

Suddenly, from out of nowhere, Milo slid in front of them, blocking their path. Cal slammed into him, hurling him backward three feet. Eugene smashed his body up against him as well, throwing him another three feet. But it was not far enough. Milo stood tall, looking down on their breathless bodies flat on the ground. Milo wasn't even winded.

"Why don't you come with me?" he said.

Connie looked down at her watch, her foot tapping beside Rebecca's. It was 8:51.

Milo walked behind Cal and Eugene out of the *Odyssey Times* building. There were several people on the street. Milo whispered "Easy does it" into Cal's ear a dozen times before they reached the gray Cadillac. The people walking didn't appear to notice them, even though Cal tried to make inconspicuous weird faces and winks at them. A couple of people made weird faces back.

Cal glanced at his watch when Milo shoved him into the Cadillac's back seat. 8:53. *Perriman wrote in the fax that he might be late coming from the airport,* Cal thought. But he knew Tarpley was probably on his way.

"Where are we going?" Cal demanded.

"You'll find out when we get there," Milo said.

"Why wouldn't he be here?" Connie said, throwing her arms up. "I mean, the man hasn't seen his true love in forty years!"

"Maybe he's just nervous and wants to get the moment exactly right," Sarah said, trying to make her feel better. But Sarah was feeling just as anxious as Connie.

"He wouldn't back out, would he?" Connie asked.

"He was always right on time when we were dating," Rebecca said. "Not a minute late, not a minute early."

8:55.

Milo turned right on Main Street, driving toward the high school. Eugene and Cal exchanged looks. Cal desperately hoped that Eugene had a plan, but Eugene's distraught look destroyed that notion.

Milo glanced in his rearview mirror. "Don't even think about making a break for it."

Somebody could be threatening Grandma, Cal thought. *If I'm going to stop that meeting, I have to escape.*

Milo stopped at the intersection of Main and Sycamore. Cal noticed the car in front of them. Streamers and shoe-polish writing that read "Connellsville Rules" decorated the back window. Large high-school boys filled the car. They were already psyching up for the baseball game against Odyssey that evening.

Cal glanced at Eugene and raised his eyebrows. He had an idea.

Milo had his window half-open. Cal took a deep breath, leaned forward, then shouted as loudly as he could in a deep voice, "Connellsville is a bunch of wimps!"

The boys in the car in front of them jerked around violently like they had been attacked by a yellow jacket. Milo spun around, ready to scream at Cal but stopped short when the Connellsville boys climbed out of their car. Cal pulled Eugene onto the floorboard.

Three huge boys stomped toward the gray Cadillac. The light turned green, but they still kept coming. Car horns blared all around them.

"What did you say, old man?" yelled the biggest boy.

"I— I didn't say anything," Milo stammered.

The boy growled, "Step outside."

"I'm kind of in a hurry," Milo said. One of the boys opened the front door. Milo whimpered. It was Cal and Eugene's chance to make a break for it.

Cal tapped Eugene on the shoulder, and they crawled out the back door. They were four blocks from the gazebo.

Connie looked at her watch again. She was averaging five looks per thirty seconds. It was 9:00. She saw Rebecca look up and stand. Her gaze was far off, and Sarah followed it.

A man on foot emerged from behind a row of trees. Connie moved toward Rebecca, and Sarah joined, not thinking about the awkwardness of their presence, only caught up in the moment.

The man wore a black suit.

"Is it him?" Sarah asked.

"I don't know," Rebecca said.

Eugene and Cal sprinted into McAllister Park. Cal felt a dull pain as the crisp spring air rushed into his lungs. Cal saw a man in a black suit approaching the gazebo. His grandmother stepped forward, toward the man. The man in the dark suit smiled nervously.

As they got closer, Cal began to recognize him. *It's Alan Tarpley! What is he doing here? Is he here to hurt my grandmother?* His eyes were fixed on Rebecca.

"Hyah!" Eugene shouted.

"Ugh!" the man said, as a torpedo-like Eugene wrestled him to the ground.

"Mr. Tarpley, you are under citizen's arrest! You have the right to—"

Eugene didn't get to finish his sentence. Tarpley easily rolled him over and pinned him to the ground.

Connie gasped and covered her face. "What are you doing, Eugene?"

"Rescuing all of you," Eugene struggled to say, while Tarpley applied forearm pressure to Eugene's chest.

"What's the matter with you?" Tarpley said, with Eugene struggling underneath him. Cal ran out of the bushes and jumped on Tarpley's back.

"Ow! Get off me!" Tarpley yelled.

Connie ran forward. "Cal stop it! Stop it!"

104

"You won't get away with this!" Cal yelled.

"Hey!"

"Cal! Get off of him!"

"Ow! Stop biting me!"

"I've got him!"

"Connie, call the police!"

"Adam?" Suddenly, the brawl was over. Rebecca's lone, soft voice somehow echoed decibels over the screaming. She smiled and squinted at Tarpley.

Tarpley, on all fours with Cal riding him like a horse, leaned upward. He said, "Rebecca."

Cal's arms went numb, and he fell to the ground. Eugene shook his head. Tarpley stood up and slowly walked to Rebecca, his arms hung limply by his sides. He stopped in front of her, and they studied each others' faces.

"How'd you know it was me?" Tarpley asked. The man standing in front of them looked nothing like his yearbook picture.

"Your eyes," Rebecca said. "I always thought they went on forever. They still do."

Eugene sat up and hit himself in the forehead. "Wait a minute. Alan Tarpley is Adam Barry?"

"You look beautiful," Tarpley said.

"I've changed a bit," Rebecca said, still smiling.

"I've thought of you often," Tarpley said.

"How long have you been in Odyssey?" Rebecca asked.

"Two years."

"Why didn't you tell me?"

"I'm sorry. I was a coward. I knew you'd hate me for leaving . . . and dying . . ."

"But you didn't die."

"I wanted to." Adam looked at the ground and began his story. "Someone paid me to write the article that got me fired. It was totally fake—I made the whole thing up. When the truth came out, no one would hire me, so I enlisted and went to Vietnam. So many horrible things happened there . . .

"I knew this guy named Alan Tarpley. He was a good guy—didn't have a family though, or anyone back home. Alan died in combat. I was right beside him, held his hand. And when it was over, I switched our dog tags. A part of me wanted to die.

"I got beat up pretty bad in the war myself. They had to rebuild my face. After the surgery, I looked a lot different. Then I grew a beard. The war changed me, and Alan's identity gave me a chance to start over . . . or so I thought.

"I heard your husband died," Adam went on, "I'm very sorry. I've thought about you a lot. I wanted to talk with you, but I was afraid. But then I read your letter in the newspaper. Suddenly the past wasn't important. I needed to see you. I needed to tell you I'm sorry."

Eugene interrupted. "But why did you create the obituary that you showed to Cal and myself?"

"I wanted to keep the truth hidden. I'm so ashamed of what I've done—all the people I've hurt. But when

106

I thought that Rebecca might still love me, I couldn't bear to keep up the charade. I'm tired of living a lie."

Rebecca opened her arms, and Adam gave her a hug.

Cal suddenly grew nervous. Adam's story made him think of his own lies. What would he say when Adam asked about the necklace? Was Cal ready to give up his charade?

Eugene approached the two lost loves, still locked together. "Excuse me . . ." he said, clearing his throat.

"Eugene, whatever it is, let it go," Connie said.

The couple didn't appear to hear him anyway, so he tried to get their attention again. "Mr. Barry, Ms. Pastorini . . . "

"Eugene, what is it? Leave them alone," Connie said with clenched teeth.

"I apologize. I know this is awkward, but if I may, I believe we will soon have company, and I would rather not be here for their arrival."

Adam broke the embrace. "Who?"

"William Perriman and Milo Biltmore."

"Perriman is coming here?"

"We found a fax he sent you. He's on his way from the airport right now. And we left Milo Biltmore four blocks away just a few minutes ago."

"Biltmore and Perriman . . ." Adam said with a look of fear. "We gotta get out of here."

The Decision

April 20, 9:09 A.M.
McAllister Park

've got a car!" Connie shouted, and they all ran toward the parking lot.

Eugene caught up with Connie. "Do you have six seats?"

"We'll have to squeeze," Connie said.

"Are there six seatbelts?"

"Five."

"State law requires all passengers to—"

"Fine, Eugene. You can sit on the roof."

When they made it to the parking lot, Connie came to a quick halt at the curb. "I thought I parked right here."

"What?" Eugene said. "You lost your car?!"

"Rebecca, Sarah. Don't you remember? I parked right here."

108

"You obviously didn't, Miss Kendall. Unless your car is microscopic, in which case, I don't see how the six of us—"

"Quiet, Eugene. Let me think."

"Uh oh," said Cal.

"Uh oh, what?" Sarah asked.

"There's my car," Connie said.

"Where?"

"Right there," Connie said. She pointed to her left. A blue compact sped toward them. Cal turned to run away. But another car flew toward them from the opposite direction. It was the gray Cadillac.

Milo Biltmore was driving Connie's blue car. He stopped in front of them and leaned his head out the window. "Looking for this?" he asked. Behind Cal, the gray Cadillac screeched to a halt. "Three of you hop in here," said Milo. "The rest of you get in the Cadillac. Senator Perriman and I are going to take you for a ride."

Adam was insistent that everyone abide by Milo and Perriman's wishes. He knew them better than anyone there. Connie, Rebecca, and Cal piled into Connie's car with Milo, while Eugene, Adam, and Sarah climbed into the Cadillac with Perriman.

"Where are we going?" Cal asked.

Milo ignored him and continued driving.

April 20, 9:28 A.M.
Trickle Lake Park

The cars pulled into the Trickle Lake Park entrance. Milo parked on the shoulder at the beginning of a trailhead, and Perriman followed him. They forced everyone out of their cars and onto the trail. Cal wondered why they were heading to such an out-of-the-way spot—but then quickly decided not to think about it.

Milo and Perriman lead the six of them into the woods.

"All right, this is good enough," said Perriman.

"Why'd you bring us out here?" Cal demanded.

"I don't want any scenes," Perriman said. "This is a nice, quiet place, don't you think?" Perriman stepped closer to the group. "Adam. My friend Adam . . . what happened to our pact?"

Adam didn't blink. "When things aren't right," he said, "you have to fix them."

William frowned. "Three days ago we were a team. What happened since then to ruin our friendship?"

Adam stood firm.

"You know what," Perriman continued, "I think I know what happened." He stepped toward Rebecca. "I think *you* happened, Ms. Pastorini. That was quite a letter." Rebecca stayed quiet.

110

He turned back to Adam. "So love made you do this, huh, Adam. I'm disappointed in you. It used to take much more than this to make you abandon your convictions. No offense, ma'am," he said, glancing at Rebecca.

"Why don't you get on with it, Bill," said Adam, stone-faced.

"Fine," Perriman said. "Give me the letter."

Eugene spoke up. "The police have it."

"I want every copy," Perriman said.

Everyone was silent. Cal's hands shook at his sides. He could feel the bulge in his back pocket where the copy of the letter was stashed.

"I can make your lives miserable," Perriman said. Milo smiled, and his torso stiffened.

"I've got the only copy," said Cal. He pulled it out of his pocket.

"Excellent," said Perriman, and Cal handed him the paper. Perriman unfolded and looked at it, almost fondly. "Ah, the memories. Seems like only yesterday, huh, Adam?"

"There's still a letter at the police station," Adam said.

"Oh, don't worry. I'll get that one too. I didn't become a senator without knowing some important people."

"I can still prove you did it," Adam said.

"But you won't," Perriman said.

"What makes you say that?" Adam asked.

"Because you love your life too much. If you tell the press or the police, you'll lose everything. Plus, when the police find out you stole someone else's identity, they'll throw you in jail. So just forget this. Then you can go back to being Alan Tarpley, and I'll go back to being vice-president of the United States."

"He'll turn you in," said Connie. "Adam doesn't want to lie anymore."

"People don't change as much as you think," Perriman said. "His life is so full of lies, he wouldn't know what to do with himself if he tried to be virtuous. If he tells the truth now," said Perriman, "everyone will hate him all over again. He'll relive the pain. No one will forgive him for the rest of his sorry life."

"God will, Adam," Connie blurted. She looked him in the eye. "Ask God. He'll forgive you. I forgive you."

"So do I," said Rebecca. "I forgive you."

"Adam doesn't want to start over," Perriman said before Adam could answer. "He's an old man. You get used to living a lie."

"No, Mr. Perriman," Rebecca said. "I watched Adam become a Christian. Adam, you changed your life once before." Adam stared at the ground.

Rebecca continued. "When the Birches's home burned down, you spent every weekend that summer helping them rebuild it. And I remember the first time you taught second graders in Bible school. Johnny Philips had trouble reading, and you worked with him as much as he needed. Those kids loved you."

"Ms. Pastorini—" Perriman interrupted.

"And then you made a mistake," Rebecca interrupted back. "We all do it. And we all need to fix the things we've broken. God will let you do that. God will help you do that. He wants to be part of your life."

Adam looked up at Rebecca. "Rebecca . . . when I got greedy forty years ago and took Bill's money, it was the worst time in my life. I was ridiculed, hated . . . I lost the respect of everyone I held dear. I want you to know I love you, but I simply couldn't bear to go through that again. I'm sixty-five years old. I can't go back to the bottom. My sin, forty years ago, will follow me all the way to my grave. I can't even fathom how God could forgive me for it. I don't see any other way out."

"There is another way out, Adam," Connie yelled. "It's—"

"I believe Mr. Barry has made his decision," Perriman interrupted. "Come with me, Adam."

Adam took one last look at Rebecca. A tear rolled down her face. "I'm sorry." He turned away with his head down and followed Milo back down the trail.

Perriman stayed behind. "By the way, if any of you get the idea of going to the police, let me remind you. You have no evidence left, and I am going to be the vice-president. Who would possibly believe you?"

Perriman turned on his heel and headed back down the trail. Everyone exchanged looks of disbelief.

Cal looked at his grandmother's red eyes. Cal hadn't seen her this sad since Grandpa died. And for some reason, he also felt sorry for Adam. *If only he had confessed decades ago. I'm one to talk,* Cal thought.

Redemption

April 20, 2:36 P.M.
Home of Rebecca Pastorini

Perriman had left Connie's car on the street by the trailhead, so Connie drove everyone home. Cal got out at his grandmother's. For a long time, he hadn't wanted her to find out about the necklace. But now it was time.

"Grandma," Cal said once inside. "Do you wish you could marry Adam?"

"I did when I was very young, but we're different people now Cal."

"But you still love him, don't you?"

She nodded her head slowly. "Adam has a special place in my heart. When we were young, he said he was going to change the world. And he made me want to change the world too. But Cal, the Adam I just saw in the woods has only one goal—to keep his secret hidden. He doesn't see beyond that."

Rebecca turned around and began to dust the mantel with a fingertip. She continued to reminisce. "If he just would've confessed his sin early, he could have moved beyond it by now. He let it get too big."

Rebecca went on, but Cal was not listening to what she was saying. The words she spoke rang through his brain like a song he couldn't get out of his head: "He should've confessed his sin early. He let it get too big." Cal felt his stomach churn. *If I confess it now, I can take my punishment and get it over with. If I don't, the thought that I've stolen from my grandmother may haunt me forever.*

"Grandma," he said, "I have something to tell you."

Cal and his grandma looked through the glass counter at Frampton's Pawnshop. She gazed at the necklace and smiled. "Wow," she said, "he must have really liked me."

Cal chuckled, though he wasn't in the mood for jokes. All he could think about was the disappointed look his grandmother had given him when he confessed. She told him she was proud of him for telling her, but Cal felt like it would be a long time before their relationship was the same as it had been.

Rebecca stared at the necklace. "Do you have the money?" she asked Cal.

Cal dug into his pocket and took out the three hundred dollars. Rebecca handed it to Mr. Frampton. "I'll give you four hundred for it."

Mr. Frampton considered, then looked her in the eye. "Deal." Grandma wrote out a check for the other one hundred. "You have to pay me back, though," she said.

"I will," Cal replied.

As they left the shop, a boy on a brand new XR-3000 sped by. *It's gonna be a long time before I get one of those*, Cal thought.

He looked up at his grandma. "Grandma, if I bring it right back, do you think I could borrow the necklace for an hour?"

Cal didn't want to waste any time doing what he had to do, so he ran as fast as he could to the *Odyssey Times*.

The secretary was away from her desk, so Cal walked right to the door marked "Alan Tarpley, News Editor." Cal had a feeling Adam would be there. He figured the newspaper was the only thing Adam had left.

Cal looked through the window at the side of the door, and Adam was staring out the window. Cal knocked, and Adam mumbled without looking back, "Come in." Cal opened the door, and Adam still did not raise his head.

"Mr. Barry," Cal whispered.

Adam's head popped up when he heard the name.

"I'm sorry to bother you," Cal said.

"That's okay," Adam said. "It's Cal, right?"

"Right," Cal said, digging into his front pocket. "I have something to show you." Cal cleared his throat. "The package that you sent to my grandma. There was something inside it."

Adam's eyes grew large, as if he understood.

"Do you remember this?" Cal pulled out the diamond necklace and placed it on the edge of Adam's desk.

Adam's eyes welled up. He slowly moved his hand toward it, then he picked it up and cradled it in his palm.

He whispered, "I didn't realize she never got it."

"I'm sorry I took it."

"I wanted to marry her. And I would've if . . . " his voice trailed off. "My life was going to be perfect. Everything I ever dreamed of was within my grasp. Then I got greedy. The biggest mistake I ever made."

"It wasn't your biggest mistake, Mr. Barry," Cal said. Adam looked up from the necklace for the first time. "Your biggest mistake was keeping it a secret."

Adam continued to stare at him, then a half-smile crept out. He nodded slowly. "I suppose you're right."

April 20, 5:12 P.M.
Whit's End

Cal went back to his grandmother's house and invited her to Whit's End for ice cream. When they arrived,

Sarah, Eugene, and Connie were gazing pointlessly into their ice-cream bowls. Sarah hadn't touched hers. Connie stood behind the counter, not intending to eat hers either.

A boy approached the counter asking for ice cream. Connie shuffled over her bowl, but it was already half-melted. The boy protested, but Connie glared at him and he slinked away.

The door opened, but the group did not look up.

"Rebecca?" It was Adam. "I need to talk to you."

"I don't want to talk to you," said Rebecca.

"Rebecca, I'm sorry, but—"

Connie blurted, "You opened up a deep wound and you didn't even bring a Band-Aid." Everyone turned to Connie like she had just spoken in Latin.

Adam said, "I need to tell you something. I wrote a story that's going to be in the newspaper tomorrow. It's a confession, explaining all that I did forty years ago."

Rebecca straightened up in her chair, and Connie dropped the rag she was holding. "I may lose my job. I may not be able to work anywhere in journalism. And I'll probably go to jail when everything comes out. But I figure I'll have my life back. Anyway, I wanted to tell you I'm sorry."

Without another word, he turned around and headed for the door. A stunned silence permeated the room. He was almost outside when Rebecca shouted "Adam!" He spun around. Rebecca walked toward him. "Thank you for the necklace."

Cal looked on and smiled, knowing his grandmother had forgiven Adam.

"You're welcome," said Adam. "Can I call you?"

"Please do," Rebecca said. Connie wiped a tear away with a napkin. Cal raised his hand for Eugene to give him a high-five. Eugene recoiled as if Cal was going to slap him.

"Thank you all," Adam said to everyone. Before leaving, he said, "By the way, there might have been a minor leak in this story. You should watch the news tonight."

April 20, 6:34 P.M.
Home of Connie Kendall

Everyone gathered in front of the television as the top news story came on. Cal was excited and intrigued.

"In Washington today," the announcer said, "U.S. Senator and vice-presidential hopeful William Perriman may have hit a political bump in the road. Sources say that in 1962 he allegedly paid a newspaper editor to falsify a story that would help him get elected to the State Senate. Sources in Washington have uncovered evidence that Perriman paid Adam Barry, then editor of the *Odyssey Times,* a total of $50,000 to print a false story to help him in the upcoming election."

The television showed Perriman being hounded by reporters as he tried to get into his car.

119

"Mr. Perriman," one reporter asked, "Is this your signature on this letter to Adam Barry, offering him $50,000 to write a false article?"

A clearly flustered Perriman said, "I don't know."

"You don't know your own signature?"

"It was forty years ago. Signatures change."

Another reporter shoved a microphone in Perriman's face. "Senator Perriman, do you think this story will hurt your chances of being selected as a vice-presidential candidate?"

Perriman stopped. He took the microphone out of the reporter's hand. His lip started quivering, as if this were the first time he had even considered the loss of the nomination. "I just want to tell the American people, I believe in the freedom of every American. I believe in lower taxes, a strong military . . . " his voice trailed off, and he gave up. "Oh, forget it. Just let me get to my car."

The news anchor came back on. "A more thorough investigation will begin immediately."

Connie turned off the TV. When she turned to face everyone, there were smiles all around.

"Well . . ." Cal said. "There's finally something entertaining on TV."

"Indeed," Eugene said.

A weight had been lifted off Cal's shoulders. He would sleep well for the first time in days. He imagined Adam Barry would sleep well for the first time in forty years.

Connie made dinner for all of them that night—

spaghetti with sauce—and they all sat around laughing and talking about Adam, and Rebecca, and 1962.

April 24, 7:04 P.M.
Home of Cal Jordan

Cal grabbed a thick weed and pulled up with all his strength. The ground around it loosened and a round mass of dirt came up with the roots. He shook it out and put the weed in a garbage can that was already full. He had already been doing this for four hours.

He hardly had the strength to raise his head when Sarah rode up on her bike. "Hey, Cal," she said. "What are you doing?"

"I'm grounded for two weeks, which means extra chores."

"Pretty tough," Sarah said.

"Nah," Cal said. "It's not too bad." And, in fact, Cal was serious. Normally, Cal would complain. But something had changed. As bad as it was having to pull weeds for four hours, it was not the worst part of his punishment. The worst part was knowing that he had disappointed his grandmother.

"So do you need any help? Maybe we could get this done and go for a bike ride. Your dad would never know."

"No way," Cal said. "I don't think I can take any more secrets."

Sarah smiled. "Good. I was just testing you. To see if anything had seeped through that thick skull of yours."

"What?"

"I'm kidding," Sarah said, chuckling. "Of course, it did take you a really long time to solve the mystery."

"I solved it before you."

"Eugene solved it, you mean."

"Eugene was holding me back," Cal said.

"Yeah, right!"

Then there were some things that would never change.